WHERE THE FERRY CROSSES

By
B. J. WOODS

Where the Ferry Crosses
This book is a work of fiction. The characters names, incidents, dialogue, and plot are the products of the Author's imagination or are used fictitiously. Any resemblance to actual persons or events is purely coincidental.
Copyright 1993 by B. J. Woods
ISBN: 0-9636901-0-8

All rights reserved. No part of this book may be reproduced or transmitted in any form or by any means, electronic or mechanical, including photocopying, recording, or by an information storage and retrieval system without the written consent of the Author, except where permitted by law. For information address: B. J. Woods, 825 Mt. Alban Road, Vicksburg, MS 39180.

DEDICATIONS

Dedicated to those individuals and small few who face seemingly insurmountable odds, who have courage and commitment, who believe in the system, and who, each in his own way, die a little each time waiting for it to work.

Also dedicated to that person who believed in, remained faithful to, and encouraged the Author when times were difficult. Without her this book would not have come to be. She stayed in the background, known by many, but known only to the Author for her contribution to this book.

To my Cousin Hal. Was it luck or fate during your Christmas visit that we had an opportunity to talk about my book? Regardless, your enthusiasm and professional help have proven to be invaluable to me.

SPECIAL THANKS

To Beverly, Bob, and Steve—

Words cannot adequately describe my appreciation for your interest, dedication, untiring effort and encouragement. With your help the Author has realized a lifelong dream.

PREFACE

The cotton crop has many enemies. As the seed germinates and the plants emerge through the soil, insects are ready to attack the tender growth. If these early attackers don't destroy the crop, the feared boll weevil is sitting in wait to infest the plants in early summer. An active poisoning program is necessary to kill the insects in their early life cycle. Allowing them to mature will surely lessen the farm's yield or destroy it completely.

The farmer must be vigilant and alert to this unrelenting attack and be prepared to take decisive action to rid his field of the menace.

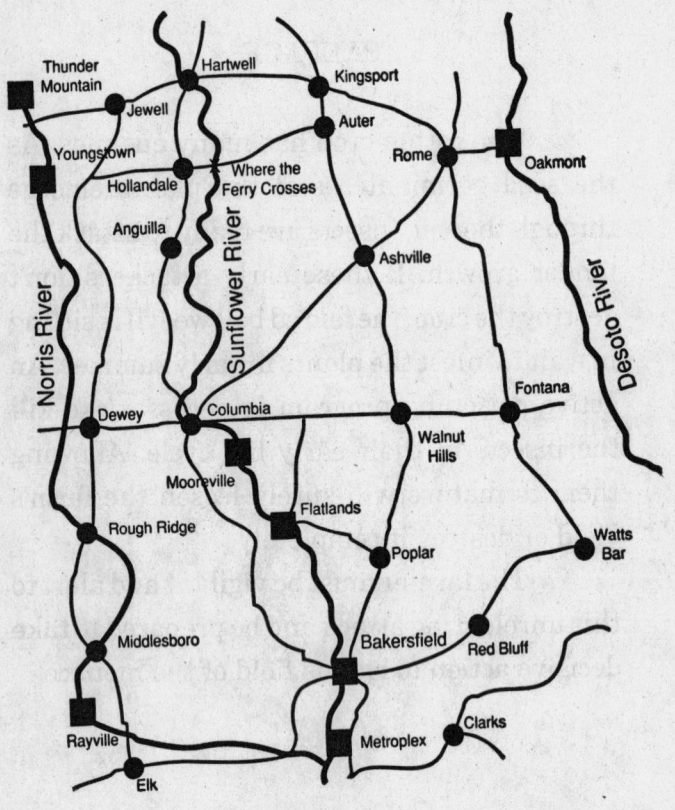

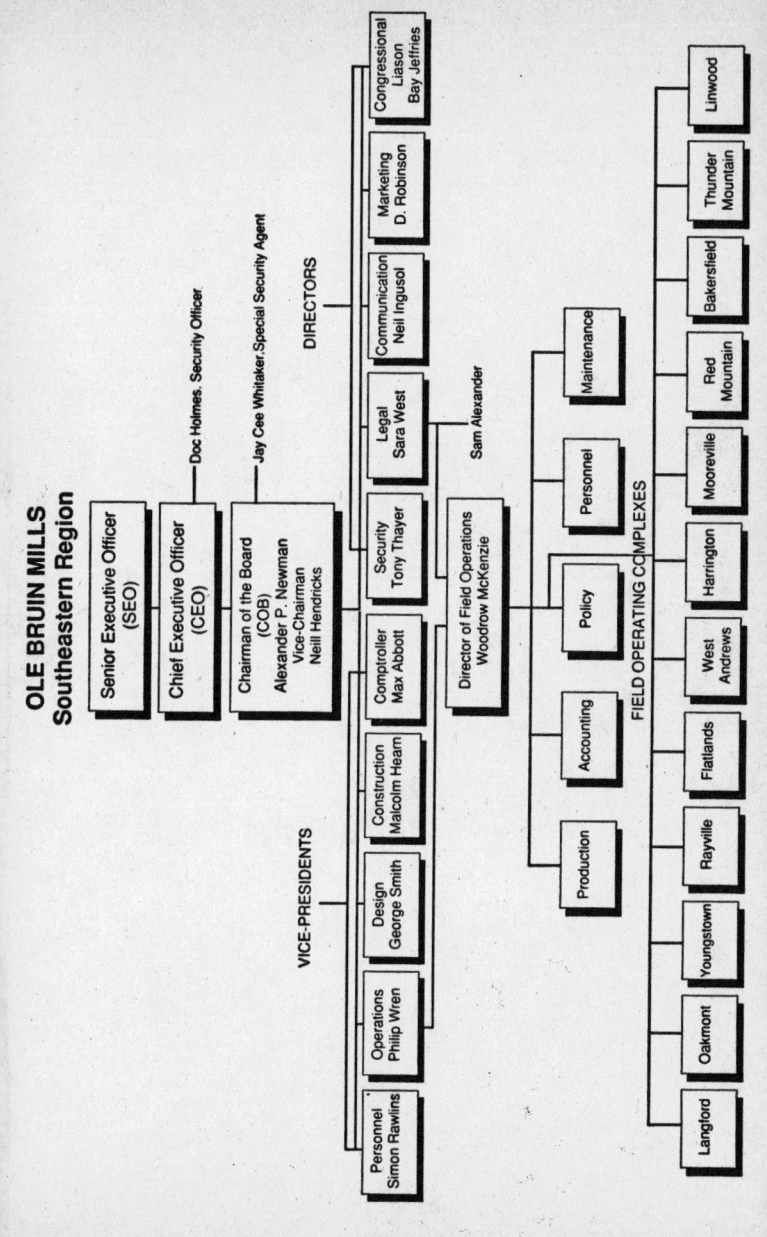

PROLOGUE

THE ODE OF THE BAKERSFIELD FIVE

It was a normal routine day, that 22 April 81
The weather was nice and the work was about done.
You were happy because you did not know
That a cloud from the South was beginning to show.

That cloud was to bring a great surprise
Much to the amazement of the Bakersfield Five.
On to the complex and thru the gate
Rode Doc and Sara in their sedan V/8.

Sara had been advised to ride and read
However she could only ride and plead.
"I must have a coke," was her cry
"If I don't get one, I will surely die."

They rode to the house with a bang.
Then Doc yelled, "Come here, Nange."
Sara knew this action was for real and no joke
When Doc threatened Nange with a stay in the poke.

Next it was time for the Farmer to reminisce
And Roberta's time to kick and hiss.
Bobbie Sue said, "I don't believe a word"
And Nancy replied, "That's absurd."

B.D. and The Kid were waiting in the wings
Trembling with fear and afraid not to sing.
Daniel was making notes as calm as ever
For he knew that this was a truthful endeavor.

                    B. J. Woods

                    © 21 Mar 91

1

It started out like any spring day. Woody McKenzie got out of bed at 5:35 a.m. as usual. He looked out of the window toward his mothers' house one hundred yards away. The light from her kitchen window reflected on the dew covering the joining yards. He sleepily stumbled into the shower feeling the warm, soft water rolling down his shoulders. He could hear the other family members preparing for the day ahead. He stepped out of the shower catching his reflection in the mirror. At forty Woody was proud of his athletic look. His 220 pounds tapered down his six foot two inch frame. Broad at the shoulders and slim at the hips, he sported a full head of brown hair which complemented his dark brown eyes. His long strides were positive proof that every muscle in his body was in tone.

Woody heard Allison, his six-year old daughter, turn on the water in the other bathroom. The smell of Cappuccino filled the house. Woody smiled thinking of his wife Martha in the kitchen fixing breakfast. He could hear the sound of bacon frying and his mother at the kitchen door with a pan of homemade biscuits. Everything was normal. Woody sighed thinking of the mundane routine of his life. With all the impatience of an eleven-year old, Woody's son Barry yelled, "Hurry up Allison!" Joseph, the oldest of the three kids ran down the steps. Soon they were all headed to school and work. It was just another typical day in the lives of the McKenzie family.

Woody pulled out of the carport and drove around the circular drive toward the blacktop road, looking back with pride at the house he and Martha had built. With his car rolling along the newly paved surface at a relaxed pace Woody was thankful for the peace and solitude of country living. Three years earlier he and Martha had packed up the family and moved from a crowded subdivision to forty acres of rolling hills, hardwood trees and green pastures.

As Woody entered the city limits the rising sun reflected off of the skyline of Walnut Hills. The traffic was light and Woody had no trouble making the eight mile journey and entering his assigned parking space. The six story office building was quiet as usual. After greeting the usual group of early arrivers, talking about the weather and how cold the morning was, he went to the comfortable, fifth floor office he had occupied for thirteen years. Woody had barely settled at his desk sipping a warm cup of coffee, looking over the stack of paperwork when the day took an unusual turn. The phone rang twice signifying an out-of-town call. He lifted the receiver and answered in his usual monotone voice, "OBM, Woody speaking".

The gruff voice on the other end of the line said, "Don't try to recognize my voice or ask my name. Just call me Candor." The sternness in the voice surprised Woody.

"Okay, I'll listen."

The speaker began to tell one of the most bizarre stories Woody had ever heard. "Since you've been a long-time faithful employee of OBM, this situation needs your special attention." Woody was stunned as the man relayed the recent activities at the Bakersfield complex. The Bakersfield complex, about 135 miles south of Walnut Hills, is a remote public utility constructed and operated by the Ole Bruin Mill Corporation.

"Why are you reporting this to me?"

"I trust you to take action to clean up a cancer that is about to destroy the company."

"Why me? Shouldn't you be calling security?"

The ten-man OBM security department has the mission to receive complaints, investigate and provide corrective steps to the Chairman of the company. The caller's voice changed, losing some of the sternness. "There is no one else I know at OBM who can be trusted as much as Woody McKenzie. Please don't try to identify me."

"I give you my word I won't try to speculate who you are."

"If you want to verify any of this you can talk to Bakersfield community leaders and your own employees at the site."

Woody listened in stunned silence as the mysterious caller unfolded an unbelievable story of mismanagement, seduction, and murder. All the allegations of crimes pointed to Lawrance Wilson.

Woody said, "This is impossible! Lawrance Wilson? Lawrance has a degree in criminal justice and law enforcement."

"This is only the tip of the iceberg Woody."

The informant had extensive knowledge of company organizational rules and policies. He told Woody if an investigation did begin, OBM officials must be prepared to deal with distribution of illegal drugs, misuse of company resources, misuse and abuse of personnel, sexual misconduct, violence, theft, and murder. Woody grabbed a pen and furiously scribbled as the caller continued to talk.

"I'll call again when it's necessary and safe. Remember, Woody, I'm counting on you."

Before Woody could respond the line went dead. As he gently replaced the receiver Woody pushed away from the desk, beads of perspiration dripping down his shirt. Loosing his tie he stood struggling for air, heart pounding. His mind racing through the conversation. What had he done to earn such trust?

Still shaken Woody walked down the busy hallway to the restroom hoping no one would notice his stressful condition. Splashing cold water on his face he met his gaze in the mirror as his mind drifting back to early childhood days in the late forties and early fifties. Life was simple but hard.

Since summers in the deep south are hot and humid, everyone looked for a cool place to sleep. Woody's mother let him move his bed onto the screened porch surrounding their house. Even though the porch was cooler, the weight of the steamy delta air made sleeping nearly impossible. He usually made the move in early spring and didn't return until Thanksgiving.

From the porch he could watch the sky light up as spring and summer thunderstorms rolled across the sky with brilliant bolts of lightning. During quieter times he listened to the sounds of the night creatures. Every night he heard the owls hooting and fish jumping in the Sunflower River.

As the summer passed into autumn, the thunderstorms became less frequent and Woody's favorite time of year approached. Cotton was king and harvesting time gave him the opportunity to make his own spending money.

On those early autumn days as the cotton matured on the plantations of the wealthy delta farmers, ten-year-old Woody left his bed before dawn and headed to a nearby field for a long day's work.

The field was only a quarter of a mile from home, so young Woody would run in the early morning darkness, get his cotton sack out of the wagon, and start picking. The farmer always hung a special sack near the scales so Woody wouldn't lose any time searching in the darkness for his sack. All the sacks looked alike except the short child-size one which fit his short, thin frame. The white denim-like sacks were seven to twelve feet long, coated on the bottom side with tar for dragging through the cotton field. A 3-inch wide strap held the bag onto the picker's shoulder with the opening under the right arm. The average adult picker could bag two hundred pounds, working from sunup to sundown earning $2.00.

The plantation owner stood on one of the cotton wagons looking over his field. The crop being harvested was the reward for his hard work beginning with planting operations in the early spring. The lush green crop that grew through the summer had turned to a sea of white, bordered by narrow tree-lined strips. Throughout the field pickers went about their activities with zeal and vigor. The hot, dry September sun lowered the humidity and chased away the summertime insects. Its rays beamed down on the cotton, drying it and causing a sweet aroma to rise over the field.

Starting to pick just as the sun rose in the east, Woody was soon joined by other cotton pickers. In his short life, the little boy had never managed to pick two hundred pounds of cotton in a day even though he worked to exhaustion. He did know that the earlier he got to the field, the more dew the cotton would have on it. And the more dew, the wetter and heavier the cotton would be at the scales. By the time the sun was an hour long in the sky, the cotton field was full of boys and girls, men and women, black and white. It was a way of life that had existed in the south for many years. This simple life taught one to work hard to be rewarded.

An old black man by the name of Muggy O'Leary usually picked cotton in the row next to Woody. Muggy's large frame showed the years of hard work. His weather worn face, although toughened by the delta sun, radiated kindness to Woody. The little boy was always glad to see the old man. The two worked side-by-side, Muggy picking three rows to Woody's one. Muggy would teasingly encourage Woody to speed up, occasionally adding cotton to Woody's sack. About mid-morning Muggy's deep voice would spread across the cotton field as one-by-one the other field hands joined in. The soothing, rhythmic chorus kept the workers moving along at the same pace. The pickers were always singing and happy, making each other feel good when they completed a row.

Working alongside Muggy was a daily adventure and an education in the subtle lessons of life. One hot afternoon Woody could feel a thunderstorm coming and he was picking as hard as he could. The heavy air held a stillness over the field. With Saturday only two days away, he had only picked three hundred pounds of cotton all week. As Woody crawled down the row he hit a brick with his knee and saw an opportunity to add to the weight of his pickings. Grabbing the brick, he dropped it into the sack, pushing it to the bottom so it would ride easier as he moved down the row. He didn't know Muggy was watching. They continued to pick side-by-side until weigh-in time at the end of the day.

As usual Muggy, much bigger and stronger than Woody, picked up the youngster's sack and hung it on the scales. He turned to the boy and said, "Hold up the end of your sack."

Woody was puzzled because his place was always up in the wagon emptying the sacks.

"Your sack sure feels strange, boy, do you know why? Cotton don't weigh that much, something's wrong with your sack. We want to give the farmer a fair scale. He works hard to plant and cultivate his crop. We only want pay for what we've picked. The farmer deserves pay for his labors too. If we aren't honest with each other then we can't trust each other."

Woody looked down and turned away, ashamed that Muggy had caught him.

"Boy, I know you want to get ahead, but this ain't the way to do it. If you want it that bad you should go to work for your grandfather's company."

Woody was puzzled. "What do you mean?"

"You don't know about your great-grandfather, Willis Mckenzie, Sr.?"

Woody replied, "No, Mother told me a long time ago never to ask my Daddy about him.

She said I would find out about him later."

"Willis, Sr. started his own business shortly after the end of the Civil War. Willis, Jr., your grandfather, took over the business in the early twenties and turned it into a big successful company. Didn't you know your grandfather either?" I know you're still young, but I'll tell you the story of OBM, your great grandfather's company."

Over the next couple of days while picking cotton, Muggy told Woody about his grandfather and great grandfather; how Willis, Sr. had the foresight to realize that this expanding country of ours would need massive fuel supplies. "After the Civil War, there were very few jobs. Since your great grandfather didn't own much land and wasn't in the cotton business, he had to find another way to support his family. He started with a wagon, a pair of draft horses, a crosscut saw, and several axes. To the best of my knowledge, Mr. Willis, Sr. was the first person in this county who cut, split, and delivered firewood. Practically all of the homes at that time used wood burning stoves for cooking and wood burning heaters in the winter time. Mr. Willis was a hard working man who recognized an opportunity and took advantage of it.

"Before the turn of the century your family had expanded its operation to include logging and lumbering. Did you know, those big cypress trees near your house where you play were planted by your great grandfather? His philosophy was, 'If you cut a tree you should plant ten to replace it.' Back then, your family cut those big cypress trees to make lumber. Most of the houses in this country were built from lumber cut at the McKenzie sawmill. I'm sorry you didn't get to know your ancestors because they were hard working people.

"Woody, when I was about your size, I used to work in the woods with Mr. Willis, Sr. He taught me to give a full day's work for a full day's pay and that's the same lesson I'm trying to teach you. You have the same hard working spirit he did, so all you need to learn is to be completely honest."

With a puzzled look on his face, Woody asked, "I don't know anything about my grandfather's company; why didn't my father go to work for them?"

Muggy hesitated before continuing. Finally he said, "Your father, Trey, inherited the name and plans were to bring him into the company, but he was never as dedicated as his father and grandfather. He had been given the good life and did not want to start at the bottom, learn the business, and work his way up. He wanted to start at the top and boss all of the company's employees. His father and grandfather feared his attitude would mean the end of the company's rapid growth and success and could begin its decline. Willis, Sr. and Willis, Jr. gave Trey an ultimatum. He could either start in the woods as a day laborer working Saturdays, holidays, and during the summer months and work himself up or strike out on his own. Trey refused to lower himself to the life of a day laborer and severed all ties with the family.

"By the mid-twenties automobiles were making a big impression on this country. Willis, Sr. and Jr. saw another golden opportunity. They moved to Texas and used the money they had made in the lumbering business to purchase equipment needed for the exploration of gas and oil. Due to their hard driving personalities, this venture was also prosperous. It seemed like everything that Willis, Sr. attempted was destined for success. The oil and gas fields produced huge quantities and returned millions of dollars for investments in other areas.

"Reflecting back on his early childhood, Willis, Sr. once said, 'I want to be a cotton planter and cattle rancher.' The success of the oil and gas business gave him the opportunity to branch out and move into the cotton and ranching business."

All the time Muggy was telling Woody the McKenzie family history, he continued to pick cotton and encouraged the boy to keep up. Woody, although he could not possibly comprehend all he was hearing, did not understand why his parents had not told him this story.

"Where are my great grandfather and grandfather now?"

"Both died in a plane crash in nineteen thirty-nine. They were flying from Dallas to

Jackson, Mississippi, and were caught in a lightning storm. The plane went down killing both of them, two company officials, and the pilot."

"What happened to the company?"

"It's still going strong today and continues to grow. Your father tried to get involved with the company after his father and grandfather died, but there was no way. He had disassociated himself more than twenty years earlier so there was no connection he could make to reenter and gain control. The company has grown so large that stock holders control it and dictate its direction."

"Surely my father got something."

"No, Woody, there was too much anger in the family for so many years."

After the death of Willis, Sr. and Jr. company lawyers took control and effectively eliminated all reference to the McKenzie family. Willis, Sr. had been an astute businessman who knew how to make money and in the early years, was able to take care of business day by day. However, the company grew into a large corporation, and he was forced to depend on and trust his legal advisors to take care of business. The lawyers maneuvered the corporation out of McKenzie family control.

The OBM Company Willis, Sr. started at the end of the Civil War was, eighty years later, selling off some of the smaller subsidiary companies it owned and was rapidly developing into an international public utility corporation. OBM was constructing and operating multi-purpose complexes in the United States and several other industrialized countries.

The corporation developed into an impressive three-tier organizational structure. Functional managers at all levels were called vice-presidents. International corporate headquarters were located in Washington, D.C. with regional headquarters scattered throughout the United States and foreign countries. Regional headquarters were usually split into subordinate area management units. A senior executive officer (SEO) headed the international headquarters; with regional offices supervised by chief executive officers (CEO); and area management units headed by chairmen of the board (COB).

Educational disciplines and skill levels of OBM employees ran the entire gamut from the most highly specialized doctoral-degree research scientists downward to uneducated day laborers.

The SEO frequently served on economic development panels for the President of the United States. He and the organizational vice-presidents were recognized as experts on a wide range of world issues and provided input to congressional sub-committees.

The success of the OBM Corporation was excellent testimony to its ability to recognize and satisfy needs using a cost-effective method. An example of its ability was found in the national development of nuclear power. OBM Corporation officers recognized the rapidly increasing demands for energy in the twenties and thirties. They realized that the finite fossil fuel supplies could be exhausted by the end of the first quarter of the twenty-first century. Their research and development division began to look at alternate sources of fuel and played a major role in developing modern-day nuclear power technology. OBM continued to expand its global role and became quite heavily involved in environmental protection activities.

The lessons in trust and honesty Muggy taught Woody in the middle of those hot cotton fields stuck with him. The anonymous caller's unquestioning trust caused this early boyhood lesson to flash through Woody's mind. Little did Woody realize as he stared at his reflection how hard it would be during the next ten years to find others who had developed similar trustworthiness. Woody dried his hands and walked back to his office.

2

Philip Wren was nervous. "Already eight o'clock," he groaned. The plans for construction of a new complex in Louisiana lay open before him. His meeting with the Chairman to review the plans was only thirty minutes away and he knew he was unprepared. At this moment Woody burst through the door. Philip looked up.

"We have a problem, Mr. Wren."

"Well, I don't have time to hear it right now Woody."

"I know you have a meeting with the Chairman and I think you will want to discuss this with him."

Looking first at the plans, then Woody,

and finally at his watch, Philip sighed. "Okay, you have two minutes."

As Woody hurriedly related his conversation with the anonymous caller he could sense the anxiety surfacing in Philip.

"Who told you this? When did you hear it? How much do you know?" The room filled with tension as Philip fired questions at Woody.

"I got an anonymous call first thing this morning accusing Lawrance Wilson."

"We better go see the boss."

Organizationally the Chairman of the Board, COB, occupied a position two levels above Woody. He had one vice-chairman and several vice-presidents reporting directly to him. Woody reported to Vice-president Wren. The vice-presidents were organizational specialists who occupied positions as personnel officer, operations officer, comptroller, and construction officer.

After Philip called the chairman, the two hurriedly walked the two short blocks to the chairman's office continuing to discuss the allegations.

Upon entering the office they sat at the long conference table.

The Chairman asked, "What's going on?"

Philip looked at Woody. "Tell him what you just told me."

Woody again relayed the allegations he had received earlier in the morning.

After hearing the story he stood and walked to the window. As time dragged on and the Chairman continued to stare out the window, Philip turned to Woody and whispered, "Have you told me everything? Who else knows? Is anyone else implicated?"

Before Woody could answer, the Chairman turned and demanded, "How did this happen, Philip? You know we have never had a major scandal at OBM? We're going to take care of this immediately. I will contact the CEO to discuss the situation and request the assistance of his chief investigator. I want someone who will be totally objective. Clear your schedules, I want both of you available."

The investigation was underway within forty-eight hours from the time Woody received the first call. As the investigation moved forward, involving more people and more allegations of illegal activities, Woody discovered he could not trust anyone at OBM. As the allegations were discussed in larger groups, albeit still behind closed doors, those in positions of responsibility and authority rapidly began looking for ways to end the investigation. One-by-one members of the OBM hierarchy were brought into the confidence of the Chairman. It was turning into a no-holds barred, dangerous situation involving high officials at OBM.

Deals to end the investigation were suggested by the vice-presidents. They feared that if the investigation continued, their past activities and ascent to power would come under scrutiny which they could not endure. That one anonymous phone call on a cold March morning might, in the end, reveal a much larger group of individuals who had committed numerous and possibly more significant crimes.

Pressure was being placed on that boy who had picked cotton with Muggy thirty years earlier. As greater leverage was applied to conduct a thorough investigation, everyone involved began to ask themselves if the end result would be worth the price. The general consensus was that higher ups at OBM had more courage than lower level personnel. This thought was quickly dispelled as it became evident that the truest courage was repeatedly displayed by those of lower rank who had less organizational protection. It also became evident that the fates of those individuals rested with their knowledge and commitment to stand up and be counted. They believed in a code of ethics and a high standard of conduct.

As the investigation continued, the group of committed persons slowly began to grow. This group, dedicated to correcting the wrongdoing, became affectionately known as the "White Hat Gang" and later the "Bakersfield Five." The core group was known as "Three-M." By early May, preliminary decisions had been made which resulted in several deliberate moves within OBM. Little did Woody realize that these moves marked the beginning of a test of his courage and intestinal fortitude.

3

Woody's best friend, Jay Cee Whitaker, was a black child, who came with his mother to the McKenzie home every day. As they walked along the dusty field road in the early morning, his mind would race back to the plans he and his friends had made the evening before. Everyday was filled with new adventures as they played on the banks of the Sunflower River. Lying on their backs, looking up at the sky, the friends imaginations knew no boundaries or limitations. They played with Woody's toys under the shade of Spanish moss hanging from huge cypress trees in the yard while their mothers worked side by side in the house cooking, cleaning, and washing clothes.

During this same time a young, black girl who had been abandoned by her family came to live with the McKenzie's. Mrs. Ethel McKenzie, Woody's mother, having been orphaned at an early age herself, understood how the little girl, Ida Bee Williams, felt and took the child into the McKenzie home. Woody's father, Trey, spent hours at the end of each day teaching Ida Bee the three R's. Although she had separate living quarters, the girl soon became an accepted member of the family.

Living in such a rural area as they did, it was always a treat for everyone to go to town on Saturday afternoon and stay late into the night. The country folks called it "going to the front." Trey McKenzie operated the ferry and drove the school bus. Each and every Saturday at 3:00 p.m., he hung a closed sign on the ferry and cranked the old school bus for the trip to "the front." Ethel, Woody and his two black friends, sat up front as Trey drove the same bus route on Saturday that he did Monday through Friday except on Saturday he picked up parents along with their children. Woody's job was to open the door and let the passengers load on. Ethel collected ten cents from each person and chatted with them, catching up on the latest happenings since she saw them the week before. They always began the trip about three in the afternoon and by six o'clock arrived in Hollandale for a night on the town. Woody could go to the movie, get a coke and a box of popcorn for twenty-five cents. He often wondered why his two friends were forced to stand in the balcony while he sat in a chair on the main floor.

Only later did he learn the meaning of the word "segregation" and how it applied to white country folks just as it did to the black folks.

One Saturday after the movie let out Woody and his two friends met at their usual spot in the dimly lit alley.

"Did ya'll see that dead body that washed up on the shore? It scared me to death."

"Yes, I saw it and I'm still shaking. I wanted to leave but Jay Cee wouldn't let me."

"Ya'll are a bunch of 'fraidy cats. That didn't scare me."

The three friends started on their way through the alley to the Sterling Five and Ten Cent Store. The Hollandale merchants kept their stores open late on Saturday night to take advantage of the country folks weekly trip to town. As the children neared the end of the alley they could hear voices behind them.

"Do you let your pets stay at your house? Do you let them sleep in your house? Why don't you leave your little monkeys here? We want to have a zoo!"

Jay Cee whispered, "Let's get out of here quick." The three grabbed hands walking faster with every step. A group of teens circled Woody, Jay Cee and Ida Bee keeping up the pace.

Some of the older boys had been drinking beer and a few were already drunk. They continued circling, gesturing with their long necked beer bottles.

"We're going to get you and your little pets, pour beer down your throats and all over your body." Several members of the group laughed and clapped their hands at the idea of the punishment the three were about to receive.

Woody could hear a female voice over the noise of the crowd, "Leave your pets here and nothing will happen to you, little boy. I'll put you on the bus." Woody refused to release his friends' hands. The trio struggled to get through the closing circle, turning the corner, heading down the last block to the bus. Suddenly, one of the bigger boys lunged, locked on to Woody's thin arm and began to pull him away from his friends.

"Leave us alone!" Ida Bee screamed hysterically. The scared little girl's piercing screams caused the boy to relax his grip on Woody's arm. As he jerked away Woody grabbed the hands of Ida Bee and Jay Cee, running from the group at full speed. They covered the last block just as the bigger boys were closing the gap. The three jumped on the bus with Woody struggling to close and lock the door as a beer bottle smashed against the side of the bus.

The mob pounded on the bus door. Ida Bee, Jay Cee, and Woody crawled under a seat,

Ida Bee still screaming, and Woody praying over and over for the immediate destruction of the crowd.

The arrival of the grown-ups scattered the unruly mob. Woody's parents, usually the first to return to the bus were surprised to find the children on board. Still shaken, Woody described the terrifying ordeal. After hugging Woody to calm his fears, Mrs. McKenzie leaned over and hugged the still sobbing Ida Bee to thank her for her courage and for taking care of her baby boy.

Thirty years later Woody McKenzie would remember the episode and the courage displayed by Ida Bee. This gave him the strength to face overwhelming odds.

4

As the winter afternoon gave way to early evening Ethel and Ida Bee were hard at work in the kitchen. Ethel was fixing hot biscuits and gravy for supper and Ida Bee was doing her homework at the small breakfast table near the stove.

Ethel was surprised to hear a knock at the front door. Wiping her flour-covered hands on her apron, she headed for the front door saying, "Who in the world can that be at this time of day?"

"Beats me," muttered the little girl. Five seconds later Ethel was shouting, "Come see who's here!"

Not really interested Ida Bee casually strolled through the living room until suddenly she recognized their unexpected guest and ran toward her.

Ethel and Ida Bee were overjoyed to find Ida's half sister, Edna Claxton, standing on the screened porch.

As they hugged, laughed, and shed tears of joy Ethel said, "Come in, join us in the kitchen for some iced tea."

"Oh, that would be great. I've got a lot of catching up to do since I haven't been home in five years."

"We've missed you and always wondered if you were okay in the big city."

"We had some rough times, but thank goodness the whole family is there to help each other. We make more money there, but the groceries cost much more."

"Well, don't worry about the groceries or anything else for a while. You can stay with us. We made a garden this year, and I have plenty to send back with you. How long will you be here? Are you moving back? You know, we can find a house for you if you want to come home."

"Ethel, I really miss seeing you and being here, but I believe I'll have a better life in Chicago. I'll come back to visit whenever I can."

"Will you stay with us tonight?"

"No. I'm going to stay with Aunt Emma in Hollandale. I'd like Ida Bee to go with me for the night if that's okay."

"Sure, that will be fine. Ida Bee hasn't seen Emma in a couple of weeks. But first I want you to stay and have supper with us."

"I'd like that and afterwards we'll go to Hollandale. I want Ida Bee to wear her prettiest dress because I'm going to take some pictures."

"That would be great. I just made her a beautiful print dress. I was saving it for Christmas but this is close enough. Okay then, it's settled. Now tell us about the big city."

"Mose and I live in a big apartment house with Mamma and our four sons."

"Don't tell me; let me remember their ages. Leonard is twelve, Philip is ten, Mose, Jr. is nine, and Robert is seven."

"Ethel, You've got a good memory."

"How are Mose and the boys doing?"

"They're fine. Leonard is making straight 'A's' in the seventh grade and works part-time. The other three are doing okay but need to follow the example Leonard is setting."

Ethel laughed and said, "I know what you mean. I've got two sons and Woody would surely do better if he followed Walter's example. Maybe someday he will. That's enough talk about boys. Let me tell you about our girl. I swear Mr. Willis spends more time helping Ida Bee with her homework than he does his own two sons. Edna, you know he's not one to show much emotion, but when it comes to Ida Bee, he's a big teddy bear. It's wonderful having her with us."

"When we left five years ago we didn't have a place for Ida Bee. Mamma knew you would take care of her, but she still feels guilty for leaving her behind. When the opportunity came for us to move to Chicago, Mamma had to make some hard decisions. She knew she would have to work and couldn't possibly care for a three-year old baby."

"Edna, I'm sure your Aunt Emma would have taken Ida Bee in. But when she told me all of you moved to Chicago leaving the baby behind, I gladly volunteered to take her. Emma agreed and we got a beautiful little girl of our own to care for. Come on now, let's get supper started. I'm getting hungry and Mr. Willis and the boys will be in here starving to death in an hour."

After supper Edna and Ida Bee left for Hollandale. Two days passed with no word from the girls. Ethel was worried and insisted that Walter drive her to Hollandale. When they arrived at Emma's house no one was home. Ethel said, "Let's go to the Sterling store so I can finish my Christmas shopping; then we'll come back to Emma's in a couple of hours. I'll leave a note on the door so they'll know we're in town and looking for them."

"That's a good idea, Mother. I bet I can find a present you can buy for me."

"I've already bought your present. I need to buy a shirt for your daddy and a pair of socks for Ida Bee."

After two hours of shopping they returned to Emma's house. The note Ethel left on the door was gone, but still there was no one at home. She was getting a little bit concerned and went next door to see if the neighbors knew anything.

John Mackey answered the knock and invited her in.

Ethel asked, "Have you seen Edna and Ida Bee?"

"Yes. They visited us a couple of nights ago right before they left for Chicago."

Ethel was stunned. "They went to Chicago? Ida Bee went too?"

"Edna said they were going to drive straight through and would probably get there in twenty-four hours."

"John, do you know where Emma is?"

"I saw her leaving about an hour ago headed toward town."

"Thanks, John. I'm headed that way to find her. If she comes home, will you please ask her to wait until I return." With that exchange, Ethel ran outside, jumped in the car, and hurriedly backed out of the driveway.

Walter asked, "What's going on?"

"Edna and Ida Bee have gone to Chicago."

"Chicago? Why did they do that?"

"I don't know, but if I can find Emma maybe she can tell us."

For the next three hours Walter and his mother searched every street and store for Emma with no luck. With night approaching and almost at a point of exhaustion she said, "Walter, we need to go home. Your daddy will be worried about us if we're not home before dark."

Ethel was heartsick as she drove down the gravel road toward home. She wondered why Edna had done such a thing without telling her.

When they got home she told Willis what had happened. He too was stunned but tried to calm Ethel. "We can contact the sheriff and report this as a kidnapping, but I don't think he will do anything."

Ethel said, "I agree. It probably won't do any good. Maybe the best thing to do is wait a few days and see if Edna contacts us. If we could find Emma maybe she could tell us something."

At that moment someone knocked on the door. Willis opened it and to his surprise Emma was standing on the porch. He asked her to come in and called to Ethel.

Emma said, "Ethel, John told me you've been looking for me."

"Yes, I have. Can you tell me what happened to Edna and Ida Bee? I know they went to Chicago, but I don't know why they left so suddenly without telling me."

"Well, Ethel, Edna and her family felt terrible about leaving Ida Bee five years ago. She knew you and Mr. Willis had become so attached to the little girl that you wouldn't let her go to Chicago if you knew about it. She asked me not to tell you until they had time to make the long drive. She said, "I'll write Ethel and tell her why we want Ida Bee to be with the family and apologize for the way I took her."

5

There was a small group of employees at the Bakersfield complex who faced what appeared to be insurmountable odds and they were no doubt frightened. These people had worked for OBM many years and remained loyal to the organization. Knowing their position was the right one they were not hesitant to express themselves and take a position that defended OBM. It was Woody's self-appointed duty to support and encourage them by his actions and by constantly reinforcing and reassuring them. Extreme courage would be required for all of them to take the actions they needed to take as a matter of conscience. They were all honest, hardworking country folks who would sooner or later come face to face with the city folks. Countless hours were spent soul searching individually and in small groups trying to maintain the courage necessary to stand up and be counted.

As employees of OBM they had all taken oaths to expose wrongdoings and take whatever action was necessary to correct any wrongs that had occurred and prevent their recurrence. Each of them knew of situations and actions that had been taken against those who had lived up to the letter and intent of their oaths. As time went on it became more a matter of principle and concern for the integrity of OBM than concern for the extreme pressure and adversity each individual would have to bear. Strong friendships and mutual respect developed among members of the White Hat Gang.

The bonding reminded Woody of friendships rooted in childhood athletic competitions. After all the cotton was picked in the fall, the ginning completed, and the late fall and wet winter weather set in, interests turned to basketball. Chores in this season were fewer and the changing of the seasons in the northern hemisphere made the days grow shorter. More and more time was spent indoors and a favorite meeting place was on the basketball court.

There were usually ten or so boys and twelve to fourteen girls who wanted to split up and play. Sometimes, when there were not enough boys to make two teams, the girls were allowed to join in and play with them. When the girls joined in to make two five-man teams, the boys played less aggressively. But a friendly bump was always permitted. Young Woody always thought the boys planned those close encounters. Later in life, he realized the girls made the plans and the boys just executed.

It often seemed that the best male athlete played against the best looking female. After playing like this for a couple of years at ages twelve and thirteen, couples began to emerge. They were all close friends and enjoyed playing sports together but knew the unspoken rule - a boy could ask only one particular girl for a date on Saturday night. As a result of this long-term association, relationships between most of the boys and girls generally became more like brother and sister. Although several of these relationships developed more, there was not enough excitement to endure in adulthood. As time went by some of the girls dropped out, but most the boys went on to play high school basketball.

Nevertheless, during those teen years, the boys developed a second sense about their teammates and learned to understand and predict each other's actions in various situations. The team was successful in winning State championships. Little did Woody know that these teen relationships and lessons learned would be an enduring strength a quarter of a century later. Since that time he had believed that fate pulls individuals into groups at particular times to solve big problems or accomplish great feats. The problems he was exposed to in the spring could not have been solved if any member of the Bakersfield team had not been in the right place at the right time.

Team members were diverse in physical

appearance, family background, educational, experience, worldly exposure, and marital status. One common trait was their overwhelming sense of honesty. It was composed of three distinctly different groups each possessing different pieces of information relating to questionable actions by Lawrance Wilson. Two of the groups were made up of employees working at the complex while the third included two women and two men apparently associated with Lawrance in a more social setting. These four individuals never identified themselves to Woody but continued to provide information that added irrefutable facts relevant to the investigation. Their information was provided over the phone at all hours of the day and night. It was apparent that someone in their group knew where Woody was at all times. Their clandestine methods and identity remained a secret to the other groups.

Based upon information they provided, it was apparent that they knew the other group members and that the women in the group had what appeared to be a personal, romantic interest in Lawrance Wilson. Some of Woody's group members thought Lawrance's wife and two girlfriends were jealous of each other. Each time one of the women called with additional information she impressed Woody with her clear and soft, yet deliberate, voice. Although none of the females ever confided in Woody regarding their personal involvement with Lawrance, he sensed a strong love entanglement. On many occasions, Woody felt like the women were getting back at Wilson, not wanting to kill him, but seeking revenge for the way they had been treated.

The other groups, whose team members were known to all, were colorful collections of individuals. They had been brought together by fate to carry out a mission.

The investigator, Doc Holmes, was a hard-driving, direct, and, strangely enough, caring individual. He had a great sense of humor and extremely high regard for his own investigative ability. He was overbearing and very intense with a strong desire to seek the truth and expose corruption. He was skilled at intimidation and making guilty people squirm. He loved his job and did it well.

The legal advisor, Sara West, assigned to the case was a brilliant, logical, and law abiding attorney. Her only fault, if she had one, was that she trusted people to be honest.

There was another person in the group known as Billy Mack. He always wanted to "clean somebody's plow." The youngest member of the group, Tim Huxley also known as "The Kid," was a photographic genius and was able to secure incriminating pictures conducted by Lawrance Wilson. He was frequently in the right place to take compromising photographs of Lawrance involved with young girls. These under-aged females were described by The Kid as "San Quentin Quail."

6

As a result of the anonymous call to Woody, decision makers at the highest levels in OBM began to explore their options. It was apparent from the outset that a harsh penalty must be imposed if the charges were proved. Personnel experts and lawyers were directed by the Chairman to review the evidence. The Chairman told them that this case should be there number one priority until it was completed. Intense efforts must be exerted to ensure that the action taken must produce evidence that could stand up in court.

After a reasonable period of time to review the facts and make a judgment, the lawyers and personnel experts reconvened to present their findings and recommendations to the Chairman. Supporting documents and decisions were presented before the discussion began. After less than an hour of discussion, a consensus was reached.

The Chairman directed that steps be taken without delay to proceed with the approved plan of action. He continued to provide detailed instructions as he paced around the room. At times he made personal attacks on individual vice-presidents. He assured Woody he was not mad at him because he was only the messenger. He was, nevertheless, very upset that the situation had gotten this far out of hand. He continued to pressure the senior vice-presidents becoming very abusive and at times seemed to lose control of his emotions.

The descriptive language the Chairman used to impress upon the vice-presidents his serious intent mirrored his physical approach to solving problems. Like his five-foot-ten inch frame, his remarks were lean, direct, and to the point. Every muscle in his one-hundred-eighty-five pounds rippled with the deep seriousness of the situation. The forcefulness and strength in his voice left no doubt in the minds of the vice-presidents who were ten to fifteen years his senior that he was in charge and vigorous action on their part would be demanded. He said, "You may have found your niche and think you're retired in place, but let me tell you this. I will not accept anything less than prompt attention to reaching a satisfactory solution to this problem. Your historic slow response to problem solving will not be acceptable. If I see any one of you dragging your feet or sandbagging this effort, I'll relieve you from your position with this company immediately."

The Chairman waved his hands, shouted, and accused the vice-presidents of poor management and total lack of knowledge as to what was going on in their areas of responsibility. He asked the personnel officer if the allegations against Lawrance Wilson proved to be correct, would it be proper to bring charges of mismanagement against the vice-presidents. The personnel officer found himself in a very difficult situation. He was being asked to make a cool, unemotional decision regarding sanctions against vice-presidents, several of whom had been long-time friends.

Simon Rawlins, vice-president of personnel was known as a coward who had limited knowledge regarding company sanction rules, and a reputation of avoiding confrontation. He found himself in a tough spot. He talked for five long minutes saying nothing related to the questions the Chairman had asked.

Woody, sitting at one corner of the long shiny conference table, watched the Chairman become more irritated. After listening to the double talking Rawlins, he suddenly leaped, flat-footed, onto the conference table, directly in front of the personnel officer. His voice even louder than before, he shook his finger in Simon's face. From Woody's view, it looked like the long index finger on the Chairman's right hand was going to gouge the trembling officer's eyes out.

The Chairman, squatting in the middle of the conference table, spun around and told all of the vice-presidents and the lawyer that they were all guilty of illusive and removed management. He began to ask each vice-president, "When have you been to the field to inspect your responsibilities?"

Without letting anyone answer, he yelled at his secretary who was seated in the outer room, "Get the comptroller on the phone!"

"I'm sorry he's not in the building. It's already after 7:00." This was the wrong answer.

The Chairman, now standing in the middle of the conference table, shouted, "I don't care where he is, I said get him on the phone!"

Mrs. Stevens, the secretary, nervously dialed Max Abbott's home phone number. A woman answered the phone.

"This is Mrs. Stevens at OBM, can Mr. Abbott come to the phone?"

"He isn't home yet, but you could probably reach him at Sam's Barbecue and Tavern. He usually stops there on his way home on Friday afternoons."

Mrs. Stevens called Sam's and found Mr. Abbott there.

The Chairman picked up his phone. "I

want you to get all travel records of the vice-presidents for the past five years pulled, summarized as to length of stay via location, individually bound, and on my desk by early Sunday morning."

"Why the rush? I'll have to put my travel clerk on overtime."

"I don't give a damn what has to be done to get the information! Just get it done on time." He slammed the receiver down.

At this point, the Chairman lowered his voice and jumped off the table. He slowly walked to his desk, sat down, propped his feet up, and lit a long cigar as he stared at each vice-president. "You men better pray that the comptroller's records support OBM standards for frequency of field visits." He then dismissed everyone except Woody.

"Woody, you must be wondering why I asked you to attend this meeting. I wanted you here because you are my most promising junior vice-president. The knowledge you have gained in your years with the corporation will prove to be valuable in correcting the Bakersfield situation. I'm counting on you to put all of your knowledge and courage on the line as we move through this ordeal. My experience in solving problems tells me to find the most trustworthy person and rely on him to keep the organization moving forward in times of crisis. In this case, Woody, that person is you. I hope I didn't offend you with my outbursts toward the vice-presidents. If I did, I apologize. They are a group of slow-acting senior citizens in this company. Age has taken away their hard driving initiative, and that is where you will fit into the overall scheme of our actions. I will depend on you to use your management skills to get this job done without alienating those old guys."

The Chairman went to the wet bar in his liquor closet and set out two glasses. "What's your pleasure, young man?"

"I'll take a Bloody Mary." Woody, although he had been with OBM thirteen years, had never witnessed anything like the display that had just taken place and was somewhat stunned. He didn't know what to say for fear of saying the wrong thing.

The Chairman walked over to Woody and put his arm around the younger man as they walked toward the wet bar. All the while he consoled him, telling him how much he appreciated his courage in bringing the situation to his attention. Woody began to feel better and more at ease after a couple of stiff drinks.

He continued to talk to Woody in a fatherly tone. Woody was reassured that he had done the right thing. The Chairman told him that this was going to be a difficult task. "It will probably continue long after I've moved to the next vacant CEO's position. "This shouldn't trouble you, however, since the "black book" passed from Chairman to Chairman will contain sufficient detail to keep you in the clear and provide personal, as well as legal, protection if it becomes necessary."

He wanted to know more about Woody's family, education, and the environment in which he grew up. It was at this point that Woody told him who his grandparents were. The Chairman was stunned. "I should have realized you were related to the founding fathers. The

McKenzie name is just not that common. Now I understand the animosity some of the vice-presidents have expressed about you."

"Yes, some of them act very cool and their actions border on abusive."

"Your family background and hard working reputation have put considerable pressure on them. The experience you gained and your rise through the ranks that landed you in the Walnut Hills Office has caused them to respect you, but at the same time be fearful. Their greatest fear is that you will rise to one of the vice-president's position, move to a higher position in a regional office or worse yet move to headquarters."

"I have every intention of going to the top in this corporation if I can."

The Chairman was beginning to understand why the vice-presidents recommended Woody as an interim manager at Bakersfield. "I believe they selected you hoping that you would fail. If you fail, your rapidly rising career will come to an abrupt end."

"I'm up to the challenge and will make

sure everything comes out for the good of the corporation."

"Let's go to Sam's and get something to eat."

About noon Saturday the Chairman called and asked Woody to meet him at the office on Sunday. They exchanged pleasantries about their families and what they planned to do later that afternoon. The Chairman suggested Woody might need to be gone beginning Monday for an extended period of time. The Chairman explained that he wanted Woody to go to the field, assume control of the operation, and be prepared to support Doc Holmes, the chief investigator.

Knowing that the current manager of the Bakersfield complex was a back-slapping petty politician, Woody realized that he would not be received with open arms by all the employees. In order to neutralize the control and influence that Lawrance Wilson had over those loyal to him, Woody suggested that Lawrance be reassigned to the Walnut Hills Office. He explained to the Chairman that the employees would be more reluctant to come forward if the manager remained visible in the community. The Chairman agreed and said that he would send a plane and remove Wilson from the area.

If Woody had anything at home that needed his urgent attention, it should be taken care of before noon Sunday. The ominous and secretive nature of the Chairman's phone call caused Woody some concern; however, after their discussion Friday night, Woody was prepared to do whatever he was asked. For the first time in his career, he felt like he was in the company of a strong, intelligent leader.

7

After graduating from the eighth grade, Woody had to make a choice regarding high school. The school he had always attended was being consolidated with another school thirteen miles away. Since Woody thought of this school as a city school and because he didn't like some of the city kids, he looked for an opportunity elsewhere. His older brother, Walter, had recently married and moved to Walnut Hills. Woody asked his mother if he could go live with his brother and attend school there. Mrs. McKenzie was slow to reply and Woody understood that he would not get an immediate answer to his question. He also knew not to press the issue at that time for fear that she would say no before discussing it with Walter.

Woody realized that his mother would give him an answer in her own good time, so he had to be patient. On the day he asked bedtime came and still no word from his mother. The eighth-grader had a difficult time going to sleep that night and was up early the next morning. As he sat down at the breakfast table, he didn't mention anything about moving. They had talked for fifteen minutes, and he was finishing breakfast when she said, "Oh, by the way, I talked to your brother and he said it would be okay for you to come live with him."

Woody was elated and in September enrolled in Walnut Hills High School. Shortly after school began Woody's brother was drafted into the Army and left for basic training. This left his new young housewife with the responsibility of caring for a thirteen-year-old boy, something she did not look forward to or know much about.

Woody found himself fitting into his new surroundings and making friends with ease.

One thing that made him popular was the 1948 canary yellow ragtop Ford his brother had left behind. Although Woody was much too young to get a driver's license, this did not keep him from driving girls around town and through the park.

He soon made friends with a boy who drove speed boats. The speed boats and the river were a natural attraction for Woody since the first thirteen years of his life had been spent on the banks of the Sunflower River. He and his new friend, D.H., began a friendship that would rekindle itself thirty years later. While on special assignment in Washington, D.C., Woody learned that D.H. had joined the home organization. This knowledge thrilled Woody and brought back memories of the two teenage boys riding down main street in the yellow ragtop with their arms around good-looking twin sisters. D.H. and Woody thought it was cool to drive down the streets, release the top latches, and watch the wind snatch the ragtop back.

Little did they know that serious damage was occurring to the top and the mechanism that raised and lowered it. This became really significant one night when they were driving with two girlfriends. They released the latches and the top collapsed in its compartment behind the rear seat. It was cold in late November and had been snowing most the day. The air was filled with moisture and quite chilly. None of them were dressed well enough to ride around with the top down. D.H. and Woody got out to physically raise the top only to find that it had been so seriously damaged they could not raise it.

They were about twenty miles from home, cold and getting colder. However with no choice and the snow falling harder, back to town they went. As they neared Walnut Hills, the roads became completely covered with snow. In an effort to get home as soon as possible, Woody was driving faster than road conditions permitted. This became vividly clear when they approached the first big hill. Woody was driving too fast and as he began to make a turn on the hill, he lost control of the car and slid into the ditch. D.H. jumped out and tried to push, but the car was stuck and his physical strength was not enough to move it.

Snow had accumulated about two inches deep inside the convertible and the girls were frozen and scared. The four teenagers started walking. They had walked about thirty minutes before the first car came by. They were glad to see the car until they realized it was a highway patrolman. Woody explained what had happened to the officer who was very understanding, but insisted on knowing who was driving. When Woody replied that he was, the patrolman asked to see a driver's license. Being underage, poor Woody could not produce one so his troubles were not over.

The patrolman took the girls home, then took D.H. and Woody to the Walnut Hills police station. Woody's luck began to change when the city policeman on duty found out who he was. The policeman and Woody's brother were best friends, so he took the boys home and made arrangements to have the yellow convertible pulled to Walter McKenzie's apartment.

The next day Woody's sister-in-law contacted his mother and made arrangements to move the teenager back to the banks of the Sunflower River as soon as the current school semester ended. Woody had to finish his high school career back home.

Following high school Woody had prepared himself by graduating from the State University. He had taken advantage of other opportunities to further his education by obtaining a master's degree from Michigan State University and a doctoral degree from the University of Montana, Missoula.

During Woody's adolescent and college years, he was continually haunted by Muggy's account of his grandfather's company. Once, immediately after Muggy told him about the company, Woody asked his father why he didn't work for the company. Trey McKenzie told his son to "Shut up and never mention your grandfather's name to me again. Don't you ever discuss that company with anybody." After receiving the sternest lecture of his life, Woody was sent to bed and told to forget what Muggy had said. "Never, never discuss the company with Muggy or anyone else again!"

Woody had always wanted to know what was wrong with the company, but was afraid to ask anyone. He was even afraid to ask his mother and older brother. His father's lecture made a deep long-lasting impression on him.

Although Woody was only ten years old, he never forgot about the discussion with Muggy and the stern lecture from his father. Likewise he didn't forget about the company. He spent most of his high school years hoping someone would tell him something about the rift between his father and grandfather. No one ever did. It was as if all of the community was hiding a huge dark secret.

When Woody graduated from high school his desire to learn more about his grandfather's company had become stronger than ever. Although his grandfather had been dead for twenty years, Woody's determination to learn more about the company was undaunted. The high school reference library and records had no mention of Willis McKenzie, Sr. or Jr. When he arrived at college, Woody thought the university's historical records of businesses in the southeast would be a good place to start searching.

After a week of settling into the routine of college life and attending classes, Woody began his search. The first few days he spent three to four hours each evening pouring over the mountain of material stored in the library's basement. On the fourth day, he hit pay dirt, finding a complete chronology of his great grandfather and grandfather's business. Just as Muggy had said, it started out small shortly after the Civil War. By the time of their deaths, OBM had diversified and grown into a major United States Corporation.

After skimming the chronology, Woody's mind was made up. He had decided on a major course of study for his college education.

Some of the detailed accounts made reference to Woody's father. A biographical sketch told of the rift in the McKenzie family. It talked about how Trey had been disowned by his father and grandfather. After reading the biographical account, Woody finally began to understand why his father never wanted to talk about that part of his life.

Although Willis, Sr. and Jr. were millionaires by any standard, the record was clear that Trey would never share in the wealth. He was kicked out of the family and forced to quit high school in his sophomore year. Trey and Ethel were married that same year. Walter wasn't born to the couple until five years after the marriage, but both Trey and Ethel had to work to survive. The only work that was available was day laborer on one of the big delta farms. They worked all week long to make a total of nine dollars. They could not afford a house and were forced to live in a surplus army tent that belonged to the farmer.

Woody wondered how parents and grandparents could treat their child so badly. Since Trey was working as a day laborer for a farmer, why wouldn't he work as a day laborer for his father and grandfather? Woody continued to learn the hard cold facts about his ancestors. They were demanding, overbearing people and once Trey refused to work in the woods, they never discussed the possibility again. Each time they needed new laborers, they refused to hire Trey. They always hired someone unrelated to the family.

After reading the history of his grandfather and great grandfather, Woody understood why his father never wanted to talk about them.

The young college student found out that after his grandparents died in the plane crash, the company had been streamlined and focused on one major business. Just as Muggy had told him some of the earlier companies had been sold. The historical records revealed that the parent company had grown into an international corporation and was doing quite well on Wall Street.

During Woody's college career he took every opportunity to follow the progress of OBM. He read financial journals and followed the stock market. Major shifts in world economic and political situations caused minor fluctuations up and down in stock values. OBM's stock value never retreated very far and over a twenty-year period had shown substantial economic gains. The corporation ranked as one of the ten best investments on the New York stock exchange.

Armed with this information Woody set his career goals. After graduating from college he began working for OBM's western region, San Francisco. Woody entered the corporation as an unknown trainee and was given the same type duties and responsibilities as all other entry level employees.

After a two-year assignment in California, he transferred to Arkansas and worked in the south central operations office in Little Rock. Woody took every opportunity to broaden his knowledge base and was always ready to transfer to any of OBM's offices. His only desire was to either expand his knowledge of the corporation or increase his salary level with each move. With each transfer came a salary increase and a move up the corporate ladder one rung at a time.

Woody worked in the Little Rock office for only a short period of time when an opening in Walnut Hills, Mississippi occurred. Moving to the southeastern region was a major step upward and provided Woody with other opportunities. It didn't take Woody long to accept the offer once it was made.

The idea of coming home to Mississippi after so many years away excited Woody. He looked forward to seeing the Sunflower River and the cotton fields of his youth. The fact that Woody was returning as a success in his family's company made the move even sweeter.

Seven days after accepting the offer, Woody reported to the Walnut Hills area management office. The office geographically controlled portions of the states of Texas, Oklahoma, Louisiana, Missouri, Mississippi, Tennessee, Kentucky, and Alabama. Woody's main area of responsibility centered on field operations in the lower central region of the United States.

During the next thirteen years, Woody spent many hours traveling to and working around the field complexes operated by OBM. He became the most familiar and trusted corporate person in the eyes of employees located at the field complexes. He was instrumental in establishing the company's health and medical programs and as a result gained the reputation as a people-oriented caring person.

8

Woody arrived at the Chairman's office promptly at noon on Sunday and found him seated at the end of the long conference table reviewing the comptroller's summaries with a look of total disgust. When Woody walked in, the Chairman looked up over his glasses and invited the younger man to have a seat.

He began to reflect on the information in front of him and decided that the problem with a large diverse organization such as OBM was personnel development ladders. It was evident that numerous individuals had risen to vice-presidential positions with only limited exposure to the OBM Corporation.

Looking out his window into the dismal gray morning, the Chairman began thinking out loud. He wanted to develop a career ladder requiring a minimum of two years service in each subordinate organization before an individual could be considered for a vice-presidency appointment. He asked Woody for his thoughts.

"It would be a great goal to set but based on corporate politics, I don't think it will work. The organization is too diverse, too complex, too stove-piped, and lacking stern direction from Washington, D.C."

Woody told the Chairman about an article he had read shortly after joining OBM titled "Can Organizations Change?" The author concluded that an organization could change if the SEO and CEO could accept the fact that historical missions were exactly that – history – and recognize that new missions were appearing on the horizon. To recognize those new missions and take advantage of them would require more than lip service. Historical hard liners would be major stumbling blocks and it would take considerable knowledge, absolute dedication, and a great selling job for anyone to redirect such an organization. The Chairman sighed and said, "We have a more immediate problem at hand."

"Woody, I want you leave immediately for your new assignment. You are to take over at the Bakersfield complex tomorrow."

"What about Lawrance Wilson?"

"He will be removed from the area and reassigned immediately. All employees at the complex will be subjected to an intensive investigation and expectations are that the outcome will reach beyond Bakersfield."

"Could you describe in detail what you expect from me when I get there?"

"I think a real shake-up will be necessary. We need to strip the subordinate supervisory personnel of their duties and reassign them to specific responsibilities. Then we will require them to report daily on accomplishments. You need to select a group of employees and assign them the supervisory duties and other duties such as timekeeping. Remind all employees that they have a sworn duty to actively participate in the investigation. If they choose not to, the alternative is to pack their belongings and go home."

This action was designed to purge the Bakersfield complex of those employees who were loyal to a powerful individual rather than to OBM. Having had limited experience in actions such as those the Chairman outlined, Woody felt like he would be all alone at the field location.

Woody had friends in the field but he was not comfortable depending on them to step forward and assist him in this effort.

The Chairman planned to fly up on Wednesday to demonstrate support for Woody and could come sooner if necessary. Woody left the Chairman's office armed with instructions and voiced support. He drove until midnight, stopped, and checked in at a motel twenty miles from the Bakersfield complex.

He arrived at the office the next morning at 6:30. The complex was a massive structure of concrete and steel that housed huge machines, control panels, and a large bay full of gauges. It was a public utility designed to control water releases contained in a huge reservoir. The water was used for municipal and industrial purposes, navigation, and public recreation.

From the street looking in, there was a foreboding view of huge multi-story buildings surrounded by an electrically charged security fence. Since Woody had come from the lowest poverty level in the state to the position of directing the activities at these huge complexes, he felt like his goals to succeed were being realized.

9

During his thirteen-year career with OBM, Woody had encountered many difficult personnel situations. He had never faced such a formidable task as he now did. Even he was intimidated by the sheer size of the complex and its impressive outward appearance. He was, however, committed to the successful completion of the job the Chairman had picked him to do, no matter what the cost.

Bakersfield employees were beginning to arrive. Normally, they would go to the motor pool and dispatch themselves to remote locations for the day's activities but today Woody stopped the foreman and told him to keep all of the employees in the meeting room. Shortly before 8:00, Woody arrived at the meeting and explained to the employees what was going on and what would be expected of them.

The room was filled with approximately fifty people — male, female, black, white — employees who had worked for long periods of time and some just hired for part-time positions. Although the temperature outside on that morning was cool, the room soon became heated. Several older employees refused to sit down, and chose to stand around the back and side walls of the room.

Woody explained the situation and what was expected of them and many of those who were standing began to talk among themselves. It became increasingly apparent that they were loyal to Lawrance Wilson and intended to remain so to the point of confusing and intimidating everyone in the room. It was also clear that the overwhelming number of employees wanted to cooperate and were eager to do so. Several stood up and expressed relief that Woody had arrived and volunteered to provide statements regarding actions that had been going on for several years.

This was only the beginning of a hair-raising chain of events over the next two weeks that grew more incredible each time an employee gave a statement. Bizarre sex stories, drug trafficking, disappearance of individuals and equipment, misuse and abuse of people, threats of personal injury and damage to personal property, and threats of reprisal were rampant.

Bobbie Sue Crowder, a member of the administrative staff, waited for an opportunity to talk to Woody privately. As the room began to empty she approached him and asked in a quiet soft voice, "May I speak to you?"

"Sure." He ushered her from the meeting room to a small office nearby.

"Lawrance overheard a conversation I had with one of the secretaries regarding problems with my car. Since it is five years old and has over one hundred thousand miles on it, and since I'm a divorced mother, I must pinch pennies to make ends meet. I couldn't afford to make major repairs on the old car and found myself in an extremely vulnerable position. I believe Lawrance sensed the opportunity to take advantage of yet another woman. He took my keys and told me he would have it checked out.

"Later that afternoon as I prepared to leave work, I realized that Lawrance had not returned my keys. When I went to his closed office door and raised my hand to knock, I heard the voices of Lawrance and Jacqueline Brick, a buxom, blonde member of the office staff. From the sounds coming through the door, it was clear that office work was not being conducted.

"Everyone else was leaving me to face the dilemma alone. My young teenager was home alone. I phoned her and told her I would be a little later than usual arriving home from work. I sat at my desk trying to concentrate on deadlines that had not been met during the day. As I sorted through looking for the most urgent bills, I realized that Lawrance still hadn't signed paperwork I had finished several days before. The sheer volume of work confronting me, coupled with the situation going on in the adjoining office really upset me. I was getting more frustrated and agitated by the minute. I tried desperately to concentrate but it was almost impossible.

"I can understand you being uncomfortable."

"Before I came to OBM, I worked at a utility company for a few years while attending night school at community college. One day I was trying to clear the most urgent paperwork from my desk in time to grab a quick sandwich and get to night class on time. I needed help from the plant manager, and approached his office. As usual his door was closed. I knocked and entered. My boss was seated behind his desk. I apologized to him for the interruption and explained that I needed his signature on some dated documents. He took his glasses off while looking up and sighed quite heavily. He was obviously tired and overwhelmed with work. He asked me to have a seat while he looked over the documents. As he scanned the pages, he asked some trivial questions. I realized he was purposely taking longer than necessary to review the documents. As I became more perturbed and began to twitch and turn in my chair, he noticed my rather excited emotional and agitated appearance and asked me to come to his desk and explain one of the documents. I thought that was kind of strange since he frequently signed these standard documents. Carefully and with a feeling of trepidation, I moved to the front of his desk. He asked me to come around the desk and stand beside him. Although he had never shown any inappropriate behavior toward me, I was aware of his womanizing reputation."

"It sounds like he had a reputation similar to Lawrance Wilson."

"Unfortunately, yes. Slowly I moved to the side of his desk while looking at the papers. As I reached the edge of the desk, he suddenly stood up, pressed himself against me and kissed me on the lips. I struggled free, slapped him, and ran out of the room. The next day I turned in my resignation and began seeking a new job.

"So you see this situation with Lawrance

and a woman in the next room reminded me of that terrible day at the utility company. I didn't know what to do. I desperately needed my car keys, but was hesitant to knock on the door and ask for them. This situation was slightly different in that Lawrance had another female employee in his office. I didn't want to cause a problem that could result in my resignation. I was divorced and trying to provide for a thirteen-year-old daughter. All I wanted to do was get my keys and leave without causing a disturbance. I stayed at my desk almost an hour past normal quitting time and couldn't wait any longer. I hoped Jacqueline would open the door to leave and give me a chance to ask for my car keys. That didn't happen, so I approached the door slowly noticing that it had weather-stripping on it to drown out sounds coming from within.

"I could hear no one talking but with my heart pounding, knocked very lightly and waited for an answer. When Lawrance answered I told him I needed my keys. After a considerable amount of squeaking springs, and movement that sounded like someone dressing, Lawrance came to the door and gave me the keys. He stared as if to shoot darts through me. My heartbeat had never been so fast. As I turned to leave the office I felt a great sense of relief. Although still shaking I was able to rush home. When I arrived, my daughter was in tears. She said a man had called and threatened to kill her if her mother ever told anyone what she had just seen. Realizing that my daughter was still uncontrollably upset, I decided we should leave the house for a little while. We drove around for about thirty minutes as I calmed my daughter's fears.

"Weren't you scared?"

"I was terrified. Before returning home I stopped by a pharmacy and picked up a sedative for both of us. I double locked the doors and the two of us slept in my bedroom that night. I didn't rest well that night but was determined not to be intimidated. Arriving at work at the regular time the next morning, I began working at my desk. I had barely settled in when Lawrance called me to his office.

Bobbie Sue was teary-eyed just describing the incident. She wiped her eyes and continued her story. "As I went in I asked Lawrance if the door could be left open but he refused and told me to come in and have a seat on the sofa. When I did he proceeded to tell me how obligated I was to him. He told me that since he had fixed my car I should be thankful and consider rewarding him for all his efforts. I told him I would gladly pay him for having my car fixed if he would give me the invoice.

"What did Lawrance say to that?"

"He laughed at me and with a sneer told me that there was no way I could pay him enough in cash. I knew what was coming next so I turned to leave his office. Lawrance told me I could leave but by walking out the door my employment at OBM would be terminated. He reminded me that he had the power to hire or fire anyone at any time at this complex. Then he asked me if I remembered what had happened to Sam Thorn and he laughed again.

"Who is Sam Thorn?"

"Sam used to work here and was fired

because he refused to build a set of storage shelves for Lawrance Wilson's deer camp. I think the firing was unjust."

"I want to talk again about Sam Thorn, Bobbie Sue, but for now please go on with your story. What happened next?"

"Lawrance told me he was the king of this mountain and there was no one at Bakersfield who could stop him. He was right, it seemed like no one had the power to prevent Lawrance from doing as he pleased. Very upset, nervous, and at this point totally intimidated, I asked what he wanted me to do. He was very blunt and told me to keep my hands on my panties so that when he called me, I could drop them without delay."

Bobbie Sue was crying harder now and had to stop her story for a few moments to regain her composure. "I'm sorry, Mr. McKenzie.

"That's quite all right. Take your time."

"Lawrance wanted to make a believer out of me. He told me the invoices for repairing my car had been paid for using company funds. Since I was the only person who signified receipt of services and authorized payments, I did not understand how that could happen. He had directed a local auto repair shop to prepare a fake invoice and keep it handy just in case it was needed. The charge to fix my car was covered by submitting the fake invoice specifying that work was done on one of OBM's vehicles. Lawrance explained that my name was on the invoice. If it were ever reported, I would be the one guilty of misuse of company funds. This absolutely floored me. Lawrance told me that when the service manager brought my car the day before he had also brought an invoice with my name.

"I couldn't believe that I had something like this slip past my close scrutiny and strict bookkeeping principles. I guess I was under so much stress that I wasn't thinking too clearly. Lawrance told me to continue working just as if our conversation had never happened. He would let me know when my personal services would be required. As I returned to my desk all of the other office girls stared at me.

"Evidently, Lawrance had told some of my coworkers that I was the chosen mate of the manager for the moment. I knew what they were thinking and needed understanding and someone to talk to. Roberta Kolb, the administrative office manager and employee with the longest tenure, sensed my need and came to my rescue. Roberta was a kind, gentle caring person, yet could be as tough as nails if the situation dictated."

"Was Roberta able to help you?"

"She consoled me and told me not to be too upset. It quickly became apparent that Roberta knew I was not a willing sexual partner for Lawrance. Roberta understood my resentment and total disgust. I just couldn't believe that I had let myself become trapped in this situation. Roberta continued to comfort me and told me this could be the last straw, the one to break the camel's back. She was older and wiser than me and thought that maybe it was time to end the terror and fear that we had all endured for so long."

After crying a few more moments, Bobbie Sue was able to compose herself. "I really didn't mean to dump all this on you your first day at the complex."

"Actually, Bobbie Sue, that's what I'm here for. Did you ever have any more situations with Lawrance or did he leave you alone after that?"

Bobbie Sue smiled through the tears. "I sort of helped him to remember to leave me alone."

10

Woody wasn't prepared for the story Bobbie Sue told him that first day at Bakersfield. Later that afternoon she stopped by his office and asked if she could continue her story.

Bobbie Sue told Woody that for the next few weeks Lawrance seemed to be satisfied with Jacqueline and did not place any demands on Bobbie Sue. Their encounter had taken place during the early fall of the year and by now fall had drifted into winter. Normally winter produced two or three storms resulting in accumulations of snow and ice on the roads. OBM had a standing inclement weather policy that kept all but absolutely essential personnel off the road. Those who needed to get to the field complex at Bakersfield were picked up at home and transported in special four-wheel drive trucks.

A heavy snow and ice storm occurred unexpectedly one night that paralyzed the community. Trees were down, roads were blocked, power lines were down, telephone service was cut off. The entire community was in a state of panic.

Bobbie Sue, realizing the severity of the situation and the needs she and her daughter had, decided to walk to the nearest grocery store. The store was about two miles from her house and after only a few blocks she was questioning the wisdom of her decision. She had walked less than a quarter of a mile when she saw one of the company's special four-wheel drive vehicles approaching.

Lawrance was driving the company truck and pulled alongside Bobbie Sue, telling her to climb in. She was relieved that she didn't have to walk all the way to the store in the deep snow so she quickly climbed into the seat. He wanted to know where she was heading and why she was out walking. Bobbie Sue said she and her daughter were out of food and she was walking to the grocery store because she didn't want to drive with the roads so bad.

He said "Great, I'll take you to the store but first we need to go to the complex and check out everything." The round trip to the complex and the check-out procedure would take about an hour and a half.

"I really don't want to leave my daughter at home alone that long."

"Look, I need you to help me at the complex. We can take your daughter to my house. My wife and kids are there and your daughter can stay until we get back." This seemed logical and since she could perform some of the essential duties at the complex, Bobbie Sue agreed. Little did she know what she would face within the next few hours.

They picked up her daughter and dropped her off with Lawrance's family. The ride to the complex took longer than expected since the roads were icy and snow covered.

When they arrived at the security fence Lawrance said, "Would you get out and unlock the gate?" Snow had piled up two feet deep and after unlocking the gate, Bobbie Sue still could not open it. "Move out of the way so I can push the gate open with the front bumper." He maneuvered the truck against one gate and began to push forward. The gate opened slowly and was finally wide enough to allow the vehicle to pass through. After the rear bumper had cleared the entrance, Lawrance got out of the vehicle and pushed the huge gate closed and locked it. Bobbie Sue thought that was strange since normally the gate remained unlocked when personnel were inside. She saw no need to close and lock the gate. An uneasy feeling began to rise inside her.

Since she had the keys to the back entrance in her hands she walked through the snow another twenty-five yards to the employee entrance and unlocked it. Lawrance followed her through the door, closed and locked it. When Bobbie Sue saw him deadbolt the door, she became very concerned and asked why he had locked it. He smiled and said, "It's just a security precaution."

Lawrance asked Bobbie Sue to go to the executive lounge and make coffee. "We really don't have time, do we? I thought we were only supposed to check the critical elements of the complex and leave. I would really like to get back home before very long."

"Bobbie Sue, I'm cold and Juanita didn't fix any breakfast this morning so I'm hungry too. Just fix the coffee, it won't take long."

She went to the lounge and fixed the pot of coffee. Bobbie Sue remembered some of the stories she had heard about Lawrance and the lounge. It was known among the workers as the place where he had many sexual encounters, and was frequently referred to as his "brothel." Lawrance came in and sat on the long comfortable sofa. Bobbie Sue went into the complex and began checking all of the instruments.

After about five minutes, Lawrance called Bobbie Sue to come to the lounge. She stopped what she was doing and headed in that direction. When she opened the door she gasped.

Lawrance was standing by the sofa completely naked. As she stood there in shock, he motioned for her to come on over. She spun around, slammed the door, and ran toward the exit. He gave chase and before she could unlock both locks, caught her. He said, "I told you once before to keep your hands on your panties and when I gave you the signal you were to drop them."

Bobbie Sue was frantic. She was swinging her arms, kicking, trying to break the grip he had on her. Much larger and stronger than she, Lawrance was able to pick her up and head for the lounge. She was screaming, yelling, and pleading for him to let her go. He just laughed and told her to shut up saying, "You're going to enjoy this." He considered himself a heavenly gift to the ladies.

Continuing to resist and as they approached the door to the lounge, Bobbie Sue remembered the coffee pot just inside the door. She stopped kicking and asked him to let her walk into the room and take her clothes off. In an effort to gain freedom she told him that she considered him to be the best looking man to ever wear pants. She said, "I want you and will do anything to please you."

Surprised by her apparent willingness and sudden change of heart, Lawrance released her and followed her to the lounge door. As she opened it, she purposely let the knob slip out of her hand, wincing as though she were hurt. He grabbed the door and held it open. While he was holding the door open, she quickly stepped through, grabbed the pot, turned, and poured the steaming coffee on his exposed genitals. Howling with anger, Lawrance grabbed himself and fell to the floor, writhing in tremendous pain.

Jumping over her fallen boss, Bobbie Sue ran to the door, unlocked it, and ran through the snow to the company truck. She jumped in, cranked it, and threw it in reverse. As she backed the vehicle toward the gate she realized it was locked. Not wanting to waste time getting out and unlocking it, she chose to ram the truck into the gate. It stopped momentarily with the resistance of the strong barrier. She revved the engine as the sound of straining metal grew louder. She continued to force the truck forward and, finally, the gate gave way with a deafening crash. As she pulled through the opening, the bumper hooked the gate and pulled down ten feet of fence on both sides.

Bobbie Sue turned the four-wheel drive around and headed for town. She had driven for about ten minutes before realizing she was headed in the wrong direction. She stopped, collected her thoughts, and tried to turn around. Since the snow was so deep, she couldn't tell exactly where the ditches were. It really didn't matter because the truck was large enough to cross the ditch and not get stuck. She turned around and headed in the right direction toward town.

When Bobbie Sue approached the complex she saw an ambulance out front with lights blinking. As she arrived at the front entrance, she stopped and asked what had happened. Six medical technicians were coming out of the building with Lawrance on a stretcher headed for one of the ambulances. At the same time she saw Daniel Mosby, the assistant manager. He asked her if she would follow them to the hospital just in case they had trouble. She agreed.

While driving to the hospital, Bobbie Sue formulated her plan of action. She did not know what Lawrance had told anyone. She did not know if he had pulled the emergency alarm or used the portable battery-powered radio. Soon after arriving at the hospital, Daniel approached Bobbie Sue and began to question her. She felt compelled to tell the truth and told the whole story. He told her not to worry, he would take her home.

Reassuring her, Daniel said, "Everything will be taken care of, try not to worry. I will call the Chairman and everything will be okay. Write down the details of the assault while they are fresh on your mind. Do you want to press charges?"

"I don't know. Do you think it would do any good?"

"An investigation will be conducted later by a team selected by the Chairman. You know, Lawrance has been involved with women in the past, and each time anyone tried to press charges, local officials would discredit her story. This time it looks like Lawrance's powerful political friends might just let him down."

Bobbie Sue remembered that her daughter was with Lawrance's family and rushed to pick her up. Mrs. Wilson had been told about the accident and rushed to the hospital leaving all of the children home alone. Bobbie Sue made arrangements for a neighbor to stay with the Wilson's two kids and she and her daughter went home.

It was about six weeks before Lawrance returned to work. Even though an internal investigation had been conducted, Bobbie Sue had decided not to press charges and the matter was dropped and filed away.

As Bobbie Sue finished telling her story to Woody she smiled. "You know, he never asked me to make a pot of coffee again."

11

As promised, the Chairman was on his way to Bakersfield and asked Woody to meet him at the local airport. When the Chairman stepped off the corporate jet, he clasped Woody's hand and greeted him warmly. He suggested that they go to a local restaurant and have a good meal before conducting any business. He wanted to talk about production rates and other mundane matters. Woody was anxious to get to the meat of the briefing, but each time he started in that direction he was diverted to another subject. Finally after more than two hours of small talk, the formal briefing began.

    Woody identified by name and position

the split by allies in personnel in the work force. Of particular interest was the split in favor of Lawrance and those remaining loyal to OBM. The splits appeared in Woody's opinion to heavily favor OBM. All female employees, ninety percent of the white males, and fifty percent of the black males aligned themselves to OBM's side of the ledger. This was encouraging to the Chairman and he expressed his desire for Woody to tell those loyal employees how much he appreciated their courage.

The Chairman relayed information that a powerful Washington politician had contacted him, endorsed their efforts and appeared to be highly upset that local officials had requested that the actions in progress be stopped. A senior Washington dignitary could exert considerable influence on OBM. What had been miscalculated by the local politicians was his interest in representing the majority of his constituents rather than a few influential special interest groups.

The Chairman said, "Woody, continue implementing the plan and keep me informed on a daily basis. Since there is a possibility that telephone calls are being monitored, all information of an incriminating nature must be discussed only over pay phones away from the complex. Likewise all written correspondence will be covered by appropriate security procedures." The Chairman reassured Woody that the resources of OBM were available to accomplish the required objective, which was to clear up this mess.

Most important at this time was to reestablish Bakersfield as a viable part of the overall public service system. The best way to accomplish this was to hire a large number of new employees. In other words, double the normal staffing level which would stimulate the local economy and further dilute the strength of those opposed to the investigation. In establishing work teams the Chairman told Woody to be absolutely certain organizational loyals worked alongside the disloyals. An equal number of new employees were added to each team. Each day the loyals would report any information they thought would be useful to OBM.

After thanking Woody for the good work he had done, the Chairman returned to the airport for his flight back to headquarters. In order to hire the number of employees the Chairman had directed, Woody called the personnel officer, explained the situation and got approval to begin hiring the next morning.

Woody worked late that night setting up a work schedule for all employees. As he left the office about midnight headed for his motel, he felt uneasy. It was a cool night with light rain falling. The road to the motel was a winding one which was not marked very well. Pulling out of the secured parking area Woody had the strange sensation of being watched. Anxiously he sped up so he could get to the motel sooner, driving slightly faster than the road conditions permitted. Approaching one of the numerous side roads along the highway, the silhouette of a pickup appeared at the intersection. When Woody crossed the intersection, the truck pulled out behind him. The rain fell harder making the already slick highway even more difficult to navigate. As he slowed, the truck closed in quickly, the roar of the engine told Woody it had plenty of power. Thinking that this was just another "good ole boy," he slowed even more to let the truck pass. The pickup slammed hard into the rear bumper of his car. Woody was jolted. Woody stomped the accelerator, fighting the steering wheel to keep his car on the wet pavement. He was driving one of the company's fleet cars that had very limited power and would not accelerate quickly or run very fast. The pickup, on the other hand, had power to spare. Once again the pickup rammed the rear of Woody's car. The hit was so hard his head was jerked back. Realizing he could not outrun the pickup, he slowed gradually thinking he would have more control if he slowed the pace. The pickup smashed Woody's car harder with every collision. He tried to time the hits by watching the headlights in his rearview mirror. When they disappeared below his trunk lid he sped up.

This game of tag went on for about ten minutes. As Woody rounded the last curve and the lights of town came into view, he floor-boarded the accelerator and sped away from the pickup. The truck stopped, turned around, and disappeared in the wet night headed back toward the complex.

With racing heart Woody pulled into the motel parking lot. Was the danger over? Driving slowly through the dimly-lit area, Woody's eyes strained to see any movement through the downpour.

When he was safely in his motel room, Woody called the Chairman.

"Hello", a sleepy voice answered.

"This is Woody McKenzie, I'm sorry to call you this time of night..."

"What's wrong, Woody?"

"I think somebody just tried to kill me."

"Are you sure? What happened?"

After Woody described the incident the Chairman asked, "Are you sure it was you they were after or could it have just been some kids out causing trouble?"

"No, I think they were after me."

"Okay, I'll send someone down to keep an eye on you."

"It's not just me I'm worried about. I don't know if Martha and the kids are safe. You know how far out in the country we live."

"Don't worry, I'll take care of them. In the meantime don't drive after dark and make sure someone from the complex always rides with you."

"I don't want to put anyone else in danger."

"Just be careful, stay in touch. Call me any time."

After a restless night Woody arrived at the complex the next morning at 7:00. He had a mountain of paperwork to do and sat at his desk most of the day never leaving the office. He returned to the motel, ate supper, and immediately went to his room and dropped off to sleep.

Several loud bangs on the door awakened Woody abruptly. He jumped up, peered through the curtains, and saw a gang standing around three pickup trucks on the opposite side of the parking area. He recognized several OBM employees. Woody called the motel manager to complain. The manager said he would call the sheriff. The motel manager called Woody back and told him the sheriff or his deputy would be there in a few minutes. Woody sat in the darkness of his room watching the activities in the parking lot through a slight opening in the curtains. About thirty minutes passed before the sheriff's car arrived. The group was getting loud and unruly.

Slowly a sheriff's car pulled into the parking lot and moved toward the crowd. Getting out of the car the deputy hitched up his gunbelt and spit tobacco juice and said, "What are you boys doing out here?"

"We're just having a little party, do you want a drink?"

"Naw, you need to move on, you're making some folks around here nervous."

The crowd broke up and the three trucks left the parking lot.

Woody got up the next morning to find that his car had two flats. He called a local service station to have the tires changed. When he finally arrived at the complex he was confronted by a large group of employees standing near his reserved parking spot. Woody got out of the car, spoke to the crowd, and went directly to his office.

He called Tommy Gaston, the foreman, in and gave him a long prioritized listing of work assignments to be accomplished over the next two weeks. The foreman told Woody he did not have enough labor to accomplish the workload in that time frame. Woody noted a degree of arrogance and asked him to sit down and talk for a few minutes. Although Woody had been instructed by the Chairman to remove Tommy from his position, he had faith in him and wanted him to remain in place. Tommy asked, "Am I going to be fired?"

"That depends on how openly you assist us and obviously upon the findings of the investigation. The information Lawrance provided concerning your cooperative farming arrangement, if proved, will be grounds for removal from your position at OBM. Did Lawrance subject you to extreme pressure to cooperate with him for his personal financial gain? If so, your actions would be explained as occurring under duress and under a threat of loss of your job."

"Lawrance's comments upset me tremendously and I assure you he did threaten to fire me if I didn't allow him to become my farming partner." Tommy told about the many times Lawrance had pressured him. Knowing that Tommy had a small but successful farming operation, Lawrance saw an opportunity to use the resources of OBM and Tommy's family operation for his own profit. Associated with the complex and under Lawrance's control was a large supply depot and maintenance compound. In addition to farming supplies such as fertilizer, fuel, automotive and tractor parts, access to the maintenance facility itself was the bargaining chip Lawrance needed. Using his status as the boss, he began to insist that Tommy use whatever supplies he wanted from the depot's stock. He told the foreman he could replace whatever he used at the end of the cropping season. This made sense to Tommy since he had been a sharecropper's son and had worked under this type overseer throughout his youth. In good faith he went about his work at the complex and picked up supplies for his personal farming operation when needed. He kept an accurate running inventory of everything he took including every gallon of fuel he used. When harvest season arrived, he had made an excellent crop.

Tommy was harvesting on his farm one day when Lawrance drove up in a company car. He motioned for Tommy to come over, and after a few minutes of praise for his hard work, Lawrance gave him a company car phone. Tommy looked somewhat surprised, especially when Lawrance said, "You don't need to come to work on a regular basis any more. Since harvest time is at hand, all you have to do is carry the phone with you. If I need you, I will call and you can come to work at that time."

Tommy was shocked. "Do I get my regular pay even though I am not reporting to work? Who's going to take my place as foreman?"

Lawrance, pushing his chest out and pulling up his pants said, "Don't you worry about the complex. I'll take care of it. You just keep farming for us." This made Tommy uneasy because it just didn't sound right.

Lawrance got back in the car and drove off. Tommy stood there, phone in hand, wondering what kind of mess he had gotten himself into. Not wanting to lose any more time from his farm work, he returned to inspect the harvesting operation.

It was not until Tommy had completed his harvesting about two months later that he came face to face with the horrible reality of his joint venture with Lawrance. He went to Lawrance and said, "I've sold my crop and I'm ready to pay my debt." He pulled out the long inventory list he had developed and asked Lawrance when he wanted to begin replacement.

Lawrance looked at the list and totaled up all the items. After discussing the prices for about an hour, he told Tommy to forget about restocking anything. This situation was to be settled by Tommy paying Lawrance in cash for the supplies. He almost fainted and told Lawrance that was not their agreement. Lawrance quickly reminded him that he had not reported to work for forty-two days, yet had received full pay for that period of time.

"You told me not to come to work; you gave me a car phone and said you would call me if you needed me. Someone else would cover for me."

"You must have misunderstood. Either you pay me in cash or we might need to have an investigation to determine how much you stole from the depot."

Tommy felt weak in the knees and finally realized that he was trapped. He could see no honest way out. He was aware of Lawrance's vindictive nature from previous situations with employees at the complex. Tommy told him he did not have that much money on him and it would take him a couple of days to get to the cash. Lawrance in a matter-of-fact tone said, "Fine. Compound daily interest at the rate of twenty-five percent starts today. Don't take too long to return with the cash." Tommy left the room visibly shaken.

Even recounting this situation to Woody two years later left him sweating and barely able to speak.

12

The fear shown by Tommy and the fear felt by Woody the night before brought back memories of an incident many years earlier on the Sunflower River. He and his father, Trey, were ferrying a family in their car across the river. It was springtime and the river was full to top bank and rolling rapidly. The McKenzie family had operated the ferry for many years and made similar crossings thousands of times. Most of the time the water was smooth but sometimes where the ferry crosses was so turbulent you wondered if you'd come out alive.

Mr. and Mrs. Turcotte and their two children were visiting friends in the community for the first time and had never crossed the river before. Trey told Mr. Turcotte to keep the children in the car because there were no railings low enough to prevent them from falling into the river.

Woody lowered the approach apron to the ferry to let Mr. Turcotte drive the car on and stop midway. He set blocks behind the wheels, raised the back apron, and told his dad they were ready to shove off.

The ferry was an ancient model that had no external power. It moved across the river by the operator placing huge wooden oars on the cable and pulling along as they walked the length of the ferry. The wooden oars had been used so many times the grooves that fit over the cable were smooth and deep. The handles had darkened with human sweat and oil.

Everything looked fine as they pushed off. Woody played with the children to make them comfortable and not fearful of the river journey. As Trey began to pull on the oar, the ferry moved slowly. They floated out of the parking bay with muddy rising water beginning to swirl around them. The rusty pulleys holding the cable to the ferry squeaked loudly. When they entered the edge of the river, the cable tightened quickly. The current in the river pushed harder against the ferry, increasing pressure on the cable. Woody and his father pulled forcefully on the oars to keep the ferry moving in the right direction. Woody looked down at the swirling water which appeared to be moving faster than he had ever seen it before.

As always when the river was on the rise it collected debris left from previous high waters. A green blanket of leaves and limbs covered the water's surface. They had oared about one-third of the way across when Woody saw Trey drop his oar and quickly walk toward the back of the ferry.

"Son, keep pulling, I'm going to try to grease the cable pulley." The pulley was making a screeching noise and was not rolling smoothly. He stuck his hand in the grease bucket, pulled out a big glob, and slapped it on the cable. As the cable moved, the grease was forced into the pulley. This was not the best way to grease the pulley, but out in the river with the cable pulled tight, it was the only alternative. Woody continued to pull on the oar as Trey moved to the middle pulley to grease it in the same way.

The ferry was near mid-stream when Woody looked up river and saw a huge log bearing down on them. He yelled to his father, "Look up!"

Trey saw the log moving rapidly toward them and yelled to Woody over the noise of the pulleys and the river, "Pull harder!". The older man picked up his oar and pulled with more strength than Woody had ever seen him use. The huge muscles in his arms and neck were straining against the force of the current.

Woody looked at the frightened family and tried to reassure them. The little group realized there was a problem although they didn't know how critical. Mr. Turcotte asked, "Is there anything I can do?"

"No, just keep everyone in the car and stay calm." Woody turned to look upstream again and saw that it was going to be impossible to outrun the log racing toward them. He had never been on the ferry when it was hit by a log so he didn't know what to expect. The water was moving so fast it was beginning to lap up on the deck. He thought to himself, if the log hits us and jumps on to the deck, we will probably sink. He thought about the two small children in the car. He knew he and his father could swim, but didn't know about the family, so he asked.

Mr. Turcotte said, "I am a weak swimmer and my wife and children cannot swim at all." By this time the log was less than twenty-five yards from the ferry.

"Do you have anything in your car that will float?" They had nothing. Other than the wooden oars, there was nothing on the ferry that had any buoyancy. The log bearing down on them, the possibility of the ferry sinking, the possibility of losing this family, and the possibility of having to swim through the fast moving water and debris struck an overwhelming fear in young Woody.

Suddenly, with a huge crash, the log careened into the side of the ferry. The car was knocked to one side as Woody heard the screams of Mrs. Turcotte and her two children and looked in the car to see Mr. Turcotte's head bleeding profusely. The impact had thrown him forward in the car and he had hit his nose on the steering wheel.

Woody screamed for his father, who was still trying to push the log off the ferry. The weight of the log and the raging current were pushing the rear end downstream. The pressure on the cable was increasing with each passing second. Suddenly the ferry gave a lunge. The rear pulley was stripped of its anchor and the rear end of the ferry swung downstream. The log pulled loose and floated away leaving the ferry hanging by the middle and front pulleys. Suddenly it lunged again. The middle pulley had stripped from its anchor also. Trey and Woody grabbed the oars and began to pull vigorously on the cable.

Woody looked at the family, still trapped in the car and screaming as the ferry lurched out of control. He yelled at them to stay in the car. Since only one pulley was holding the ferry,

Woody was afraid the family would be slung overboard. He and Trey pulled harder still on the cable, having gone more than two-thirds of the distance across the river. Both were nearing exhaustion; however, they could not stop until the ferry reached the other side and was safely anchored. Finally, after what seemed like an eternity, they pulled the ferry into the mooring slip.

Once they had it tied securely, Woody and his father sat down. All of their energy was spent. Mr. Turcotte got out of his car, his nose had stopped bleeding, his wife had calmed the children and they were settling down.

Mr. Turcotte asked Trey, "Are you okay?"

"Yes, I'm okay. I'm just out of breath. Give us a few minutes and we'll let the apron down so you can get off. Are you all all right?"

"Yes, we're fine. Don't hurry. Now that we are safely tied up, we can rest easy where we are."

Trey looked at Woody and asked, "Are you okay?"

"I'm better now." They didn't have anything to drink, so Woody leaned over the side of the ferry and took a big gulp of river water. He took his hands and splashed the water on his face and hair. Even though it was a cool day, he was red hot and needed to cool down.

They all sat there not saying much for the next five minutes. Trey tried to stand but his legs just would not support him. Woody, thirty years his junior, regained his strength a little sooner and said to his father, "Just sit there, I'll let the apron down." He did so and motioned for Mr. Turcotte to drive off and up the hill. The car slowly moved forward and easily made the transition from the ferry to the gravel ramp. The driver turned and waved good-bye to the McKenzies as he reached the top of the hill. Woody rejoined his father on the ferry. Trey had recovered and was standing looking at the broken pulley.

"How are we going to get the ferry back across the river?"

"We need to signal your mother and get her to bring the boat across."

Woody thought that was a terrible idea

and asked, "How can she paddle the boat across that swift river by herself?"

"Boy, your mother is a resourceful person. She'll find a way."

"Is there no way we can repair the damaged pulleys over here?" He didn't want his mother in that small boat by herself trying to cross the raging river. He thought it was too dangerous. Woody picked up the pulleys and tried to figure out a way to fix them. Both bolts that held them together were broken and there were no replacements on the ferry.

It was getting late in the afternoon. Either they had to fix the ferry or get someone to bring the boat across and pick them up. Trey had spare pulleys in the cable house and wanted to signal Ethel to bring two across the river. They began to yell, trying to get someone on the other side to hear them. Although Woody and Trey had strong loud voices, their cries for help went unheard.

Woody remembered a local fisherman, Mr. Watson, who lived about two miles from where the ferry was moored. He told his father,

"I'll run to Mr. Watson's house and borrow his boat."

"Okay. If you get the boat, go ahead and cross the river. You'll find the two pulleys on the lower shelf at the back of the cable house."

Since Woody was young, his energy level had restored itself from their earlier ordeal. He hit the road running and arrived at the Watson's house in about fifteen minutes. Mr. Watson was not at home. However, after Woody described the situation to Mrs. Watson, she said it was okay for him to use the boat. He ran to the river, jumped in the boat, and started across the raging water. Although there was no need to rush, his adrenaline was flowing and he was on the move.

The boat was much larger and safer than his own. Once he crossed, the big problem was how to maneuver back across to the ferry. Since Woody was upstream, all he had to do was guide the boat and let the swift currents take him across and down. He hoped that once he got to the other side, he would find someone to help him get back to the ferry and his father.

With the log incident fresh in his mind, Woody kept a close eye on the floating debris. He had very little need to paddle in the swiftly moving current. His concern was being able to steer the boat if he got into trouble and whether he had enough muscle power to maneuver out of danger. Woody knew if he hit a submerged log, he would have to ride with it down river until he could free the boat.

As Woody pushed off, the swift current immediately grabbed the boat. He began to paddle trying to steer in a diagonal line across the river. The water was covered with a layer of leaves, limbs, and other floating debris, and Woody prayed that nothing big was floating just under the surface. Although he did not need to paddle fast, he was so anxious he couldn't resist. The current looked much swifter now than when he was on the ferry. The boat began to tip and roll as he rode through the waves. The hair on the back of his neck was beginning to stand up and he felt very tense.

Woody was in a dangerous situation. He found himself facing the possibility of losing control of the boat and capsizing.

Finding something to hold onto in the event the boat turned over was uppermost in his mind. He had barely made it to mid-stream when he looked back toward the ferry and saw his father standing there watching him paddle harder and harder. Woody quickly glanced upstream to see if anything unexpected was coming his way. To his relief he saw nothing that presented any greater danger than he was already facing.

Woody was perspiring heavily and breathing even harder. As he looked straight ahead he saw someone standing on the top bank near the ferry slip. Sweat was streaming down his face blurring his vision. He quickly wiped his face and eyes with an old dirty rag he found lying on the boat seat beside him. With a little clearer vision, he recognized his mother and older brother standing on the shore. The sight of them made him feel better; however, he knew he would have to carefully guide the boat through the debris. They could not help him except to shout words of encouragement.

Woody had passed the two-thirds point and was getting very tired again. He had used up his energy supply and was surviving only on courage and determination. The young boy was so exhausted and hot he was about to pass out, yet he knew that he couldn't give up before he reached the safety of the willow grove. If he didn't keep steering the boat, the current would sweep him downstream. There was no telling what perils he would encounter if he failed to reach the bank near his mother and brother. As they watched Woody struggle, both of them realized the danger he was in as they continued to encourage him to keep fighting the river. His brother yelled, "Move to the upstream side of the boat, don't let the limbs go under your boat, make them go around, if possible."

Woody finally reached the grove of willow trees and managed to wedge the boat against one tree and hang on to another. He stayed in that position for a few minutes trying to regain his breath and cool off. Then he leaned over the side of the boat to splash some cool water on his face and arms. He took the old rag, wet it, and put it on top of his head, the water dripping down his hot face.

Walter called to Woody, "Are you okay?"

"Yes, I'm just resting for a few minutes. I've got it made now. Go to the cable house and get two new pulleys."

"Okay, but come on to the bank while I'm here watching you."

Woody had cooled off and regained a little strength so he pushed away from the willow trees and headed to the bank. The current was not as swift behind the grove of willow trees and he pushed to shore with ease. His mother ran to the boat, grabbed the rope, and tied it off. Woody asked, "Were you worried?"

"I was scared to death. I was so afraid you weren't going to make it. When your father gets to this side, I think I'm going to kill him for letting you try this."

By the time Woody's mother quit fussing, Walter had returned with the two pulleys. She said, "Wait, neither one of you is going to cross this river by yourself. I'll go get a couple of our neighbors to take the boat back across."

She was gone about thirty minutes and returned with two men. One of them said, "Y'all stay put; we know how to cross the river when it's like this." Woody was relieved. He didn't want to cross the Sunflower River again that day.

The two men pushed off and headed upstream behind the willow grove where it was easier to paddle. Just as Woody had done, they used the current to help them cross once they were far enough upstream. Within two hours Trey and the others had safely returned to the cable house. The ferry had been repaired and was ready for the next trip across.

13

Roberta had extensive knowledge related to personnel actions and was given the job of hiring fifty-plus employees before the week ended. Hiring so many people in such a short time frame was not a problem. High unemployment rates and the fact that OBM's pay scale far exceeded any other industry in the region resulted in a flood of applicants. Many applicants were already employed elsewhere but saw this as an opportunity to increase their earnings and move ahead in life. All red tape had been eliminated. Her job was to locate a source of employees. She called local employment offices and before the week ended she had hired sixty-eight new employees. Her knowledge of policy and of the community and its leaders proved to be an invaluable asset to Woody and OBM. She had worked with other managers and was a seasoned employee who got the job done.

The Chairman called and told Woody to go to a pay phone and return the call. This seemed strange. Woody drove toward town in an effort to find a public pay phone.

The Chairman said, "Our security people have advised me that the phones at the complex have been tapped.

"Do you want me to have the phone company clear the lines?"

"No let's leave them in place. That way we can feed them information when we want to."

Woody reminded the Chairman of the previous night's incident and asked that the request for a bodyguard be expedited. As they talked, Woody learned that the former bodyguard for the wife of the U.S. Attorney General would arrive at the Non-Connah International

Airport that night, rent a car, and proceed to the motel. The Chairman promised Woody that the bodyguard was a Southerner who had risen to the highest levels in the CIA. He had met the Chairman during an assignment with the CIA and had numerous overseas assignments during his eleven year career. Reservations had already been made for the bodyguard to occupy the room adjoining Woody's.

The Chairman informed Woody that his room reservation had been changed and all of his belongings moved to another room. The bodyguard was assigned to the connecting room. He would contact Woody at 6:00 tomorrow morning. Woody said, "I appreciate your concern and assistance."

The nature of Woody's job caused him to be away from home about one hundred nights a year. He tried to arrange his travels such that he could lodge at the Bakersfield Inn as often as possible. He and the innkeeper, Raleigh Walters, became good friends and frequently ate supper together. Raleigh was always interested in activities at OBM and frequently provided information from the public's viewpoint about the Bakersfield complex.

Over the years, Raleigh told Woody many stories about the local law enforcement situation. When he had approached the City requesting a building permit for the motel he had been informed that he would have to pay a small under-the-table fee to the sheriff. After several attempts to legally obtain a permit he finally gave in and donated $1,000 to the sheriff. One day later his permit was approved.

When Woody returned to the office he filled Roberta in on the status of the telephone lines. He needed her to devote all of her energies to managing the office and keeping him informed of anything she thought he needed to know. From past experience, Woody knew she kept her ear to the ground and knew everything that was going on at the complex and in the community. Woody, knowing that the company investigator would be arriving soon and also knowing that Roberta knew the employees better than anyone, asked her to develop a personnel list for the interrogation. The information she should develop must follow the procedures outlined in OBM's standard operating plan. Roberta took this assignment and along with her other duties attacked them with a passion.

During the years Woody had been employed at OBM, he had developed a good working relationship with Roberta. She was known throughout the organization as a loyal person who would exert whatever amount of effort necessary to get a job done. She had served on a committee to review management procedures which was chaired by Woody.

Shortly after returning to the office, Woody was contacted by the investigator, Doc Holmes. Tipping the scale at two-hundred-forty-five pounds and standing six feet-four inches, Doc towered over the average employee at OBM. His harsh voice and penetrating eyes were complementary ingredients to his imposing physical stature.

Doc asked Woody to meet him for lunch off-site. Realizing that the phone lines were tapped, Woody suggested meeting at a public place. This whole affair was taking on an ominous flavor. He met Doc who began to lay out the procedures to be followed for the next several days. His interrogation room was set up in a local motel and Woody would make employees available in the order Roberta suggested.

To ensure that personal rights were protected throughout the investigation process, Sara West was assigned to be present at all times. Sara's petite figure and shoulder length golden hair frequently caused new acquaintances to wonder why she had chosen the legal profession rather than a modeling career. Her soft-spoken mannerisms and physical beauty disarmed would-be adversaries and often led them to believe she was just another beautiful woman. They couldn't have been more wrong because she used her good looks to complement her razor-sharp mind.

Sara's presence pleased Woody because he had worked with her on other occasions and had great respect for her abilities as an attorney. She had, in Woody's mind, broken the stigma surrounding lawyers. Based on his association with lawyers related to organizational and personal situations, he had developed mistrust and contempt for everyone in the legal profession, believing all lawyers were dishonest and their only interest was in winning the case without regard for fair play or the truth. They were, in Woody's mind, a group of egomaniacs who thought they were the smartest people on earth. They loved to play big shot roles and enjoyed humiliating decent, law abiding, honest citizens.

Such was not the case with Sara. She was a real person, neither presumptive nor overbearing. She expressed an interest and concern for those with whom she came in contact, and her genuine, sincere personality made them feel comfortable.

Sara and Woody first met after he was robbed while on a field trip. He arrived late at his motel one night after working all day and driving eight hours. He had stayed at the same motel many times in the past and never had a problem. He was dead tired, ready for a long, hot shower and bed. He registered at the front desk, picked up his room key, and due to the lateness of the hour took only his small overnight bag to his room. He left his briefcase and suitcase in the company car never thinking that he might be robbed.

Woody had an early appointment the next day with one of the most powerful members of Congress and had requested a 5:00 wake-up call. As Woody arose to begin the day, he went to the window to check on the weather. It had been raining the night before and he was hoping the sky had cleared since the meeting with Congressman Bradford was to take place in an outside setting near the city's pecan grove. It was a favorite meeting place for politicians - open air, clean, and the perfect place for a local political favorite to meet his constituents and deliver speeches.

As Woody looked out at the bright sunlit morning he noticed that the passenger side window on his car was down, yet he had checked the windows the night before. The window was smashed in and his belongings stolen. Not only did the thieves take his suitcase, they also took his briefcase. He ran back to his room, grabbed the phone, summoned the motel manager, and called the police.

The meeting with the Congressman was scheduled for 9:00 and Woody had nothing to wear except the casual clothes he had worn the day before. That would be very improper since the meeting with the Congressman involved community leaders and the dress code was sure to be coat and tie.

When the police arrived, Woody was surprised that the chief had answered the call in addition to the patrolman. He gave them the pertinent information and explained his dilemma regarding the 9:00 meeting.

The police chief said, "We need to go for a ride," and insisted by placing his hand on Woody's arm urging him toward he car.

"Okay, if you say so." Woody was getting anxious and told the chief he did not have time to go for a joy ride.

"Calm down. We're going to open up the men's store on Main Street and find you some clothes."

Woody was relieved for he had thought

he was headed for the police station to fill out a robbery report. The chief called the store owner and asked her to meet them at the store in five minutes. It was obvious from their conversation that the store owner and the chief had a good relationship because no explanation was given and no questions were asked. Shortly thereafter they arrived at the store. Mrs. Kline, the owner, greeted them and asked how she could help.

Woody explained that he needed a suit, shoes, shirt, and tie immediately. She said, "No problem," and laid out several suits and ties for him to choose from. In less than thirty minutes they had Woody newly outfitted. Since Woody didn't have enough cash to pay for the new clothes, Mrs. Kline told him not to worry, he could pay later, whenever it was convenient. He was overwhelmed at her generosity, and thanking her once again departed with the chief.

On the way back to the motel, Woody described the contents of the stolen briefcase: confidential letters and papers he needed for the meeting with Congressman Bradford. It could prove to be embarrassing to OBM and the Congressman if the papers fell into the wrong hands.

Rather than returning to the motel the chief turned north onto Interstate 75. Woody told him that the meeting was scheduled for 9:00. The chief said, "Sit still and listen," and began to explain that he was supposed to pick Woody up and brief him on the meeting with the Congressman. Woody was shocked again for the third time and the day had hardly begun.

The chief told him that Congressman Bradford was going to assist OBM, but there was no need for any detailed discussion about the plans today. He explained that the Congressman wanted to devote more time today to his reelection effort and that Woody should attend the meeting, shake hands, make small talk, and leave.

"Chief, was the robbery a setup?"

"No, but it did provide me with a golden opportunity and legitimate cover to come by the motel and deliver the Congressman's message. There was a series of robberies along the interstate at various motels last night. Probably a small gang from the metropolitan area found the motel parking areas easy pickings." He turned the car around and delivered Woody to the pecan grove for the meeting.

After about two hours, Woody returned to the motel. When he arrived, he discovered that a policeman had taken his car to a local body shop where necessary repairs had been made. The policeman was still at the motel and stretched out his hand to shake with Woody and said, "Have a nice day." Woody thanked him for the assistance.

Woody reported to the Chairman explaining about the robbery and detailing the outcome of his meeting with the Congressman. He was pleased to hear from Woody and expressed sincere concern. He told Woody that OBM would take care of all costs related to the robbery. All Woody needed to do was contact OBM's legal division to report the robbery and complete the necessary paperwork. When Woody called the legal division, the secretary referred him to attorney Sara West. As he described what happened, Sara told him to get a copy of the police report and bring it by her office when he returned to headquarters. He explained to her that he had to visit a couple of other field units before returning. She said, "No hurry. I'll have the paperwork ready for your signature when you return."

Woody welcomed the chance to get such understanding from a lawyer and an offer to actually help him through this situation. It was nothing less than a small miracle. He completed his field visits and returned to headquarters late on a Sunday evening.

Monday morning Woody's first order of business was to meet Sara face to face and tell her how much he appreciated her help. As promised, all of the reports were ready for signature. Once signed, Sara took the paperwork to Mr. Abbott, the Comptroller, and returned with payment for the lost clothes.

All of these gestures of assistance ran through his mind when he learned Sara was assigned to ensure fair treatment for the employees involved in the investigation. Not knowing the investigator and always a champion of field personnel interests himself, Woody was concerned that employee rights might not be protected. He felt relieved and could concentrate more on his own responsibilities now that he knew Sara would represent them.

14

Woody was awakened by a sharp rapping on the connecting door of his room. He sluggishly made his way to the door and pulled it open. He was instantly wide awake.

"I always knew you were a 'fraidy cat," Jay Cee Whitaker, Woody's childhood playmate, greeted his old friend with the same big, broad smile and handshake he always had.

Woody could not believe his eyes. He had not seen Jay Cee in thirty years, yet here he stood in the doorway of his room. Woody was even happier to learn that Jay Cee would be occupying the adjoining room.

Flashbacks of their childhood antics began to flood Woody's mind, great memories of fun-filled days. After he got over the initial shock, he grabbed Jay Cee and gave him a big bear hug, asking, "How could this happen?"

"We'll have plenty of time to talk later but to maintain my cover, we can't be seen in public together. I will always be close at hand, but we won't ride in the same car together or eat at the same table in a restaurant. I will change cars frequently and tell you each morning what color and type of vehicles I will be driving that day. Don't unlock your car before it has been checked every day for any signs of forced entry, fluid leaks, tire conditions, and overall appearance. I've already dusted each door, trunk, and hood with a special powder that would show finger prints if anyone touched the car."

The Chairman had explained the situation Woody faced, and Jay Cee was going to do everything in his power to make sure nothing bad happened. If everything was okay, Woody could go about his business as usual; however, if Jay Cee discovered anything wrong he would alert Woody by phoning not Woody's room, but his own room. If the phone rang in Jay Cee's room, Woody should answer immediately and remain in that room until everything was checked.

"Is all of that really necessary? It seems like a lot of trouble."

"Do you want to stay alive? There are a lot of people involved who extended beyond the local organization."

"I was uneasy before, but now I'm getting scared."

"Don't worry, you're in good hands, Frigman. I don't know the way to the complex yet, so I'll follow you this time."

So it was time for Woody to begin the first day of his life with the protection of a bodyguard. The drive to the office was uneventful. Woody parked his car in the reserved spot. There were several company vehicles moving out of the compound. Woody waved to the employees, then went inside to the office as he saw Jay Cee driving past the entrance.

Activities at the office were following the plan Woody had laid out earlier. Roberta came in to brief him and said, "Employment papers are about fifty percent complete and by the end of the day they will all be finished."

Several times during the day Woody's mind drifted back to the reunion that occurred earlier that morning. He looked out of the big plate glass window in his office hoping to get a glimpse of his childhood friend and, now, bodyguard. Jay Cee was nowhere to be seen, though Woody could feel his presence, knowing he was watching every movement around the office building. He could not wait for the day to end so he could get more details on this guy's mysterious appearance. At 5:00, the Chairman called and told Woody he would have two more visitors within the next couple of days.

"I realize you are full of pleasant surprises; however, you have outdone yourself by sending this man to protect me."

"It was a set of circumstances that developed when your name was submitted to Washington, DC. Jay Cee had made it known that he wanted to return to the South and immediately volunteered for this job when he saw your name. Jay Cee asked me not to tell you he had been selected, and explained his past relationship with you, how you had always surprised him with new toys when you were small."

"It was truly a good reward and I want to thank you for sending him."

The rest of the workday was spent going over the personnel lists Roberta had developed for the investigator. Woody and Roberta discussed each name and why she had placed it on a particular list.

By the end of the day, Roberta was beginning to anticipate Woody's questions and in some instances provided answers before he asked the question. He felt comfortable that Roberta had put a lot of effort and knowledge into the development of the lists.

About 5:30, Woody could stand the suspense no longer. He had to leave the office in hopes of finding his friend close by. As he passed through the security opening, he saw Jay Cee's car back out of a space in the public parking area. Jay Cee blended in well with regular traffic. Woody could hardly believe it.

To know he was there was comforting to Woody.

He felt a great sense of pride in knowing this individual. Woody had always paid respect to those professionals who exceeded at their chosen vocation. As he moved into the flow of traffic, he saw Jay Cee carefully slide into the traffic three cars behind so easily he appeared to be just another motorist.

Following his same routine Woody parked at the motel and entered his room. About thirty minutes later, Jay Cee knocked on the connecting door. Woody wanted to get into the conversation he had anticipated all day long, but Jay Cee reminded him to continue following his same schedule regarding eating. They would have time later that night to talk.

Woody turned the television on and watched the national and local news. He left the room about 7:00 and walked to the adjoining restaurant. By 7:45 he had eaten and was back in his room. So far everything was going just as it had for the past two weeks. Finally Woody could talk to his friend and catch up on his life for the past thirty years.

They remembered the times they played under the big cypress trees on the banks of the Sunflower River. They had nicknames for just about everything: frogs were called "frigs," turtles were called "turkles," fish were called "pish." They remembered how their daddies would put boxing gloves on them, set up boundaries, and let them box. The big gloves were designed for people three times their size and felt more like powder puffs or feather pillows. There was no way they could possibly hurt each other, but this was fun and it still carried pleasant memories.

Sometimes Woody's old black friend Muggy would come by to watch the "match." Most of these matches occurred on Saturday morning when there was no work to be done in the cotton fields. After the matches Woody and Jay Cee would take an outdoor shower under the water hose. Later that day they would all go to town together.

Woody was very inquisitive and wanted to hear about everything Jay Cee had done since he left home. Jay Cee started telling his old friend his story. He had gone to Chicago with his family, "Life was much harder there than where we had lived." Soon after arriving up north he and his family had only themselves to depend on for survival. There was no one there to care for them as Woody's family had for many years.

"I was attacked and beaten several times on the streets. I wished I had learned to fight better during our boxing matches." The street fights gave him the incentive to develop self protection skills and later the drive to open a gym to teach those skills. He worked days and went to night school, recognizing that a formal education was the best route to follow. After eight years he graduated with a degree in physical education.

Jay Cee decided that his vocation would be one that helped kids learn to protect themselves. In Chicago, the owner of the apartment building where he and his family lived allowed him to use an empty room in the basement as a workout area. Eventually Jay Cee asked permission to use the basement room as a classroom. He explained to the building owner what he wanted to do and that if it worked he would pay rent on the space. The owner agreed and Jay Cee was up and running.

He purchased basic strengthening equipment, set up his business, and invited friends over to hear his spiel and watch him demonstrate the new equipment. Within a week he had ten students, meeting from 7:00 to 9:00 each night for ten dollars each per week. Within a month the number of students outgrew the schedule and he had to start new classes during the day.

Things were really falling into place. The basement was too small for the crowd, and Jay Cee began to look for more space, finding an old closed storage building about three blocks from his apartment. The owners were initially reluctant to even consider letting a group of black youths congregate in their building, but Jay Cee's power of persuasion convinced them that he would take total responsibility for his actions and everyone he enrolled in class. Finally the owners agreed and allowed him to use about one-quarter of the floor space, which suited Jay Cee.

He knew he was on a roll, but would have to take one step at a time. The word continued to spread. Shortly after opening the "new gym" Jay Cee began to get female applicants. He had not anticipated this turn of events and was not prepared to accept them.

Realizing that he needed to take advantage of every offer that presented itself, he agreed to set up separate male and female sessions. He needed to find a female instructor but had no idea where to look, so declared, "I'll teach the class but will not put them through the same degree of physical conditioning." He asked his mother to sit in on the first session.

After it was over she quickly told him he needed to get over his male ego. Women were just as tough as men. "If your equipment and program are good enough for the men, then it is needed and with some changes can be used by everyone." Her statement shocked Jay Cee, but he agreed to use the same exercise schedule with lighter weights and less repetitions for the women. Also she told him there was no need to have male and female classes separately.

One evening at closing time a black girl appeared at Jay Cee's door. She said, "I've heard about your gym and want to join but, I want a reduced rate."

Still going through the closing process he did not pay a great deal of attention to his visitor, saying "The rates are posted on the wall and I don't give special rates." Some of the lights had been turned off so visibility was not very good. The black girl insisted that if they were back home she could get a reduced rate. Jay Cee had not talked to anyone from back home in several years. He quit what he was doing to walk across the floor toward her. It was Ida Bee Williams whom he had not seen since she left the south many years before. Jay Cee gave her a big hug and told her she could certainly get a reduced rate in his class.

The young puppy love that began under a southern cypress tree draped with Spanish moss was about to blossom into a full-fledged adult romance that led to marriage. Jay Cee's gym and self-protection business began to really take wing. In the next ten years, he and Ida Bee had four children and achieved financial security in their business.

During this time he became interested in and joined the Secret Service and began providing protection to some of the Nation's highest elected officials and their families. He went on to work for the CIA. It was on one of these missions that he came in contact with the Chairman of OBM.

Jay Cee stopped talking about himself and asked Woody to fill him in on this case. Woody thanked Jay Cee for responding to his call for help and began to relate the situation. As he talked, he noticed that Jay Cee was taking detailed notes, paying particular attention to names. Jay Cee was interested in getting a work force profile: male, female, black, white, age, length of service and who Woody thought could be trusted. He had gathered information through the FBI and State ATF computerized files on local law enforcement agencies and local citizens.

Jay Cee did not share any names with Woody nor any of the information he had gathered. He urged Woody to be very careful of some of the local officials because the information indicated that a large drug and gambling ring existed in the communities surrounding the complex.

His information indicated that on certain midweek nights large gambling operations were conducted in so-called upstanding public businesses. He also alluded to knowledge gained through ATF files that illegal drug drops were being made in areas near the complex. Local authorities were in contact with state and Federal authorities and action was planned to conduct raids on lands owned by OBM but used as recreation areas by the public.

Woody was astounded by this information and wanted to know when and where the bust would take place. Jay Cee told him he would let him know as soon as he was notified. He also told Woody that he would need to be out of the county that night. It could get rough and possibly bloody. He expected several arrests to be made and prominent citizens to be jailed.

In addition to the gambling and drugs, he also told Woody about a high-dollar call girl operation moving down the interstate from the metropolitan area. Some of the local business owners involved with drugs and gambling were also involved in prostitution. According to Jay Cee, call girls in the five hundred to one thousand dollar range were being transported across the state line to entice high rollers from adjoining states. These high rollers would fly in, spend the night gambling and paying for sex and fly out at daybreak the next morning.

According to the information at hand, these illegal activities had been growing for the past three to five years. Time had come to put an end to this type activity, but it was going to take a major effort by several law enforcement agencies acting in concert.

Jay Cee told Woody how this community activity was tied to the former manager, Lawrance Wilson. Needless to say, OBM pay did not provide enough money to become deeply involved in these high-priced activities so

Lawrance had to find another in-road to the high rollers life-style he craved.

Jay Cee told Woody that property owned by OBM under the control of the former manager was being used as drop zones and protected meeting places for drug deals. Since OBM had its own security force, no one ever suspected that drug deals were being made under the protection of OBM. The more Jay Cee talked, the more enthralled and amazed Woody became. He asked Woody to give him a complete profile on one employee, Ben Thompson.

Ben had worked for Woody in years past so he was able to provide a rather lengthy educational and work experience background. Woody thought this interest in Ben was strange, but Jay Cee explained that he had been under surveillance by ATF for about two years and was code named "small bag man." He had been photographed several times around Bakersfield in company vehicles associating with known small time drug offenders, and had been followed on a special route delivering goods and receiving money.

None of these actions were related to Ben's primary employment with OBM. An undercover agent for the ATF had entered his confidence and had bought illegal drugs from him. Ben was paid in marked bills. None had been recovered; however, it was just a matter of time before they showed up at the gambling tables or appeared in the hands of the metro prostitutes. Ben's days were numbered, and Jay Cee believed he was not aware of his precarious situation. Jay Cee thought Ben was "feeling his oats" and getting a little bit sloppy and complacent about his activities.

"Where does the name "small bag man" come from?"

"Lawrance Wilson is 'the big bag man.' Ben makes all of the public contacts with known drug dealers and turns the money over to Lawrance. This money gives him cash to flash at the gambling tables during the mid-week games."

The same undercover agent on Ben's trail also played the mid-week games. He told Jay Cee the "big bag man" had dropped ten thousand dollars in one roll of the dice at one of the last meetings.

From the information Jay Cee gathered, Lawrance was in deep debt to other gamblers around the table and was being pressured to pay up. Since Ben's bag runs were producing only small quantities of cash, Lawrance began to look for more ways to raise money. Unfortunately his evil mind again sent him in the wrong direction.

Since OBM had a reputation of taking care of its employees a confession of his gambling situation and a request for assistance from the Chairman would have resulted in free legal advice and probably other help being made available to Lawrance. The organization would take care of him if only he asked for help. The request never came so the situation evolved to one that put two old friends together in a most unusual setting.

"Does Wilson have any personal belongings remaining in the office?"

"All of his things have been boxed up, labeled, and sent to headquarters. The only thing left is the locked desk in his office, there might be something in it."

"Has security opened the desk?"

"There's a legal question about opening the desk that remains unanswered. Our lawyers have submitted a request for ruling to a local Federal judge who will rule in the next week or so."

"Based on case history, I know how the ruling will turn out. If OBM officials think the desk contains anything in the way of evidence, then it is subject to seizure rules and can be opened at once. Will you phone the Chairman so the three of us can discuss the situation?"

After Jay Cee explained the legal situation, it was decided that the security officer would open the desk the next day so Jay Cee could examine the contents before they were sealed and sent to headquarters.

Although it was nearing midnight, the Chairman seemed pleased that Woody had called and talked to him about the situation. "Keep going along the game plan that we agreed on and if you have any trouble or concern call me from the pay phone."

Woody was concerned that the motel phone lines were tapped. "The whole community seems to be feeding off of each other so it will take some major arm twisting to get them cleared."

"No problem, a communications expert has checked the motel switch board and everything was okay. A recorder has been installed on the line to detect any listening devices. Jay Cee, you report at 10:00 a.m. and 2:00 p.m. each day. If I'm unavailable report to the vice-chairman, Neill Hendricks. Failure to do so will indicate trouble and immediate steps can be taken to send reinforcements from a special undercover squad located in the metroplex. I don't want to alarm you I but want you to be aware of everything. I have contacted the CEO. Demands to halt the investigation have been made and external pressure is being applied directly to the CEO, although he has refused to take any action to stop the investigation. He wants weekly updates. Every step of the investigation and any action taken based on the findings must be done judiciously and with the full realization that every step will be reviewed very carefully. The slightest technical violation will be grounds for halting any future personnel actions."

Both Jay Cee and Woody understood the seriousness of the conversation and pledged their total support. This situation had grown far beyond anybody's imagination and had reached the top rung on OBM's ladder. It was after midnight and Woody suggested that they call it a night and get some sleep. Jay Cee went to his room.

15

Woody arrived at the office the next morning on schedule. He watched from the plate glass window as his friend faded into the traffic in the public parking area. He began pouring over the mountain of paperwork on his desk. Roberta had set up a schedule for each employee to come in and discuss their employment contracts. He was concerned that some employees were performing duties unrelated to those previously agreed on and wanted to be sure the assigned duties, the employee's actual performance, and the employee's understanding of his contract were all the same.

Roberta had once again followed instructions to the letter and her innate ability to communicate with and understand Woody continued to be helpful. She knew what he wanted to accomplish and her knowledge made their working situation very productive. She understood the interrelationship of employee contracts and how one was a support function for another. She had organized the discussion such that downward supervisory control lines were followed.

Roberta also reminded Woody that he was scheduled to make a speech that night to a community group and had directed one of the line supervisors to prepare remarks and supporting visual aides. He had forgotten about the speech and thanked Roberta for her reminder.

Woody asked to review the text of the speech at 1:00. That would leave plenty of time for changes if any needed to be made.

With that out of the way, Roberta ushered the first employee in for his review. The first few reviews went well. Being the most highly educated, they were able to provide answers they thought Woody wanted. He was convinced however that the main office force did their job even in the face of major distractions caused by the former manager.

As he talked with the office employees, it became apparent that some were required to perform personal errands for the manager. These errands were time consuming and contrary to standard operating procedures and goals. Frequent delays in meeting deadlines were the direct result of interferences by the manager. His personal goals were placed ahead of company priorities.

Many instances of falsification of official documents were presented to Woody. Each document was accompanied by a story in which the manager controlled employees by trapping them into compromising situations.

Sexual encounters under duress in the office with more than one female in the same day caused a very stressful and tense office atmosphere to exist. Woody was amazed that such activities were conducted in the office with so many different people present and involved. Account after account told how Wilson used duress by threatening to fire someone if he or she failed to comply with his personal demands. He convinced the employees that he had full control over all personnel actions and would get rid of them if they didn't meet his demands. He was the only person at the complex who had worked in headquarters and convinced all employees that he was in good standing with important people in the top echelons. He talked as though he was a personal friend with all of them and that they had given him full reign to be the "king of this mountain."

Woody, in his interviews with the employees, tried to convince them that they had rights. The organization had rules and regulations that would ensure fair treatment for everyone. They were hired to perform a specific set of duties and they had, upon accepting their positions, stated that they would be loyal to OBM. This did not mean loyal to a particular individual whose personal financial gain was contrary to the accomplishment of OBM's goals. It meant that certain duties related to the overall operation would be performed to the highest level possible and each employee would be compensated accordingly.

However, many employees still feared for their jobs and, in some cases, for their lives. Working under this pressure and intimidation soon dictated that whatever the boss man said do was done, no questions asked.

Roberta reserved the last hour of the day for her interview. Being a strong, proud individual, she had a difficult time telling her story. She began by apologizing to Woody. He sensed that she was very upset and tried to calm her. She said, "The only way to calm me is to let the whole ugly story come out of my mouth."

She was shaking and on the verge of tears. Woody handed her a box of tissues and offered to get her a coke. She thanked him and said, "I'm fine and I want to tell my story." She waited until all of the clerical staff had left for the day because she did not want them to see her so upset. Woody tried to console her. He told her nothing she could say could possibly be any worse than the horror stories he had already heard.

"Grab hold of your chair because I am about ready to 'bust' open. I've got to let it out. Has anyone mentioned me in their interviews?"

"Yes, a few people."

"Have they mentioned my slave-like working situation with Lawrance?"

"No one has even hinted that such a situation existed."

At this point Roberta began to sob heavily. Woody felt a great deal of empathy for her. "You don't need to tell anything that is personal unless you feel it would make you feel better."

"I hope it will make me feel better, I've never told anyone what I am about to tell you. I know the clerical staff knows all of the details of use and abuse, but we don't openly discus it. Lawrance pressured all of us to have sex with him. Each time someone refused he would threaten to fire her and disgrace her in the community. His reputation as a womanizer followed him from his last two places of employment and I was aware of the extreme pressure that was going to be placed on me to perform sexually. I knew it was coming, but I didn't know how to prevent it. I didn't know how to resist it."

"Are you sure you want to tell me all of this?"

Roberta nodded and continued, "When Lawrance was first put in charge at the complex he called all of the females into his office. He told them that he wanted to get to know them professionally and personally. He told them that they would run things around the office and he would support their actions and decisions.

"He asked each one to fill out a personal profile of fifty questions that began with birth and was brought to present day. He wanted to know everything about their family, early childhood, hobbies, husbands, boyfriends, marriages, divorces, children's ages and sex, likes, dislikes, personal problems, past and present, financial situations, wants and needs. All of us talked about it and thought he was a great man. We thought he was truly interested in helping us and our families. We didn't know that we were signing a warrant that would be used to trap us. We were providing personal information that would later be used as a basis of sexual harassment and blackmail."

Lawrance had boosted their morale by telling them they could run the complex; he would make the hard decisions and take care of any disciplinary problems. All they had to do was surface the problem and he would solve it.

He convinced them that he was sincere and if they were loyal he would help them financially. If they needed money he would get them cash rewards, he would promote them, and in general, make their lives much easier.

He invited them to a potluck supper along with their entire families. Roberta began to understand at this family supper during the blessing delivered by Lawrance that something was not all it was supposed to be. In the blessing he talked about pulling together for a common cause, building on group strength, and asked everyone to support him in this effort. Lawrance told the employees if they believed in him, lined up and followed, never questioning his motives, they would be rewarded.

Roberta was wiping away tears that were streaming down her face as her beautiful red hair began to fall. She was emotionally spent. Woody, realizing the personal trauma she was going through, asked if she wanted to continue tomorrow. Since she had already stayed forty-five minutes past her normal quitting time she said, "Yes." She would like to continue at a later date. "I need to go home to fix supper for my family and house guests."

Woody looked out the plate glass window and saw Jay Cee looking toward the office. He and Jay Cee had set up a signal when he was ready to leave the office. Woody was to close and open the window blinds two times, leaving it closed as he left the room. He gave the signal and went to his car. He exited, stopped, and locked the double security gates. Jay Cee, seeing that everything was okay, pulled into the traffic ahead of Woody. Unless there was a problem, whichever one followed would drop back three to five car lengths. Woody followed the plan and sat back in traffic for a minute or so. Jay Cee pulled ahead though still in full view of Woody, keeping him in sight in his rearview mirror.

The drive to the motel took about twenty minutes; however, Woody did not have his mind on the road. He could not help but feel heartsick for Roberta. He wondered how many women had been intimidated by Lawrance. As he drove along he became more angry with each passing mile. He pulled into his usual parking space and sat with his head in his hands. He was exhausted from the day's activities and completely drained after hearing and seeing the tremendous despair in Roberta.

He was reminded of a cartoon he once saw. There were two buzzards sitting high on their perch looking down on some animals below. After sitting there for a while one turned to the other and said "Patience hell; let's kill 'em." That pretty well summarized Woody's feelings about Lawrance. Woody was sure some of the female employees died a little each time Lawrance placed his horrible twisted demands on them.

Woody finally got out of his car and went to his room. Jay Cee was already there. He had the ability to move around like an invisible man and could see that Woody was upset and asked him to share the load. Woody began to talk and was able to vent some of his pent up anger. He suggested that they go out of town for supper but was reminded that the Chairman said they should not be seen in public together. Jay Cee said, "Don't worry. I have arranged for a special vehicle to pick us up."

"I'll take a shower and get ready."

As they were leaving the room, Jay Cee told Woody to go to the motel restaurant, place an order, then go to the salad bar near the door to the kitchen. Someone would signal for him to come to the kitchen.

Woody followed instructions, and as he entered the kitchen he was met by two men dressed in grand fashion and two equally impressively dressed women. They quickly put a hat and topcoat on him and ushered him out the back door into a waiting black limo.

Woody asked, "Where is Jay Cee?" The

window behind the driver opened, the chauffeur tipped his cap and said, "The frig man is at your service."

One of the lovely ladies poured champagne into glasses held by the other one. Before they could say "bottoms up" one of the men toasted Woody. He said "I bring greetings from the SEO and CEO and wish you well. They are behind you and you will be richly rewarded. Believe that the situation is going to get worse as we move forward. We have touched a huge community cancer and more influential citizens will be exposed."

This toast made Woody feel good and bad at the same time. He appreciated the support; however, he was concerned that the situation would extend far beyond the complex. He wondered where this would end. Jay Cee crossed the state line before stopping at a rather unimpressive looking restaurant. It was an old mercantile store that had been converted to a trendy, upbeat restaurant exceptionale. Excellent food was served after good discussions and humor unrelated to the problems at the complex.

By the time the meal was completed, Woody had temporarily forgotten the problems he had found earlier in the day. The ride back to the motel took about two hours and Woody was so relaxed that he fell asleep almost immediately after he entered the limo.

About fifteen miles from the motel Woody was awakened. The two men in the limo got out and inspected a rental car parked at an interstate rest area. Woody was given the keys and told to go directly to the motel. He pulled out of the parking space and headed toward the interstate. The limo followed about one-half mile behind.

As he drove he could not believe what had happened. Where did these four strangers come from? Did Jay Cee set all of this up or did someone at headquarters make all of the arrangements? Regardless of who set it up, Woody appreciated the effort and felt much more relaxed and better than he had when he left the office earlier that evening. Woody entered his motel room, undressed, and went to bed. Usually he would turn on the TV but not tonight.

16

The wake-up call came the next morning at 5:30. Awakened from a sound sleep, Woody answered the call and began preparations for the day's activities. Following the usual ritual he arrived at the office at 7:00. As he parked the car at the complex, some of the employees were leaving the compound. One fellow seated in the passenger side of a pickup hollered, "Hey, bossman, how's it going?"

Woody responded, "Fine, thanks," and with a wave walked on to the side entrance of the office. It was reassuring to know that most of the workers were just common people trying to live their lives and do their jobs. It was funny how something as simple as an early morning greeting could restore your faith in humanity.

Just as he opened the door one of the black employees walked up behind him and mumbled, "You are one slick son of a bitch."

Startled, Woody turned. "Say that again.

The mumbler turned away and said, "I didn't say anything."

Woody told Tommy what had happened and asked whether the individual was a trouble maker. The foreman said, "No, but I'll keep a close watch on him."

Woody stayed at his desk working until 10:00 then he went to a public phone to call the Chairman. As he pulled into traffic, he saw Jay Cee fall in the usual distance behind him. Stopping at the phone, he noticed his friend drive by and stop a safe distance up the road.

"Woody, I'm glad you called. How are things going?"

"I'm beginning to worry about some of the employees. I almost had a direct confrontation this morning at the complex. It only amounted to some name calling but it could have become messy real quick."

"I'm going to call Jay Cee on the sideband radio, then patch us into a three-way conversation. Hold on a minute."

When the connection was complete the Chairman told Jay Cee to make contact in the metroplex to get a tail on that employee. "This might be the lead we need to identify the other individuals who were associates of this guy."

"Right, I'll have a tail on him by the end of the day."

"Woody, Jay Cee, both of you be careful. Things could really heat up."

Woody hung up the phone and returned to the office. Roberta knocked on his door and asked if she could have a few minutes. He invited her to come in and close the door. "I would prefer not to close the door. I only want to reserve the last hour of the day to continue our conversation from yesterday."

"I hadn't planned to conduct any interviews today but I'll be glad to make an exception for you."

It was getting close to lunch time and

Bobbie Sue stopped by Woody's office. "Would you like a tomato sandwich? Billy Mack brought some tomatoes from his greenhouse."

"Sounds great. Why don't you get on the radio and try to locate one of our employees near a grocery store to pick up some bread for the sandwiches."

Bobbie Sue made the call, then came back to Woody's office. "It's all taken care of. The bread will be here in fifteen minutes. I'll have the tomatoes sliced and ready. We have plenty of tomatoes for several other people to eat with us."

"That's a good idea. Why don't you invite the administrative staff to join us in the break room?"

Six more members of the office staff joined Woody and Bobbie Sue. As they enjoyed the sandwiches, talk turned to light conversation centering around families, hobbies, and children. One of the staff asked Woody how he could stay away from his family for so long. Woody said, "I hope this job will be completed in short order and I can return home very soon."

Woody explained that he had two sons, ages twelve and fourteen. Someone asked Woody if they played sports. He said, "Yes, they like the sport of the season, whether it's football, basketball, baseball, soccer, tennis, hunting or skiing." This gave Woody the opportunity to tell a hunting story involving himself and his older son, Joseph.

Ten-year old Joseph had hunted deer with his Dad, Uncle Walter, and Grandad since the age of three. Walter had dropped Woody and Joseph off at a deer stand known as "The Holiday Inn East." This name was the result of a plush tree stand the two brothers had built a couple of years earlier. It was equipped with a heater, sliding windows, and a small sleeping cot specially designed and constructed for Joseph.

Woody and Joseph climbed into the tree stand just as dawn broke. It was a cold frosty morning so Woody decided to light the heater. Immediately the enclosed tree stand was toasty warm. The hunters sat quietly expecting to see a big buck deer walking through the woods.

They had been in position two hours and the only sound they heard was the faint barking of hunting dogs off in the distance. Woody and Joseph were warm and comfortable. In fact, Woody was so warm he began to "rest his eyes" nodding off.

Joseph remained awake and alert while his dad drifted into a fairly deep sleep. Suddenly, Joseph spotted a deer walking very slowly directly toward them, but he could not see the deer well enough to tell whether it was a legal buck or not.

Quietly the young hunter watched the deer until he was able to see a big rack of antlers. He jumped up shouting, "It's a buck! It's a buck!" and fired his gun five times.

Woody was jolted awake by the sudden explosions of the deer rifle. He jumped up and looked out of the window just in time to see the deer disappear. Joseph was sure he had hit it.

Woody said, "Son, reload and in a few minutes we'll go look for the deer." If Joseph was right, Woody wanted to give the wounded animal time to lie down, but the youngster was anxious to get out of the tree stand and start looking. Woody tried to keep his son calm and explained why they needed to wait a few minutes.

Since this was the first deer Joseph had shot, he was anxious to find it. Woody, realizing how excited the boy was, gave in to his son's pleading. As they climbed down and touched the dried leaves below they heard a jeep coming down the road. It was Uncle Walter. "I heard the shooting and wondered if you needed any help. Did you get one, Woody?"

"No, but I think Joseph did."

"Joseph did? How big was it?"

Joseph, still wide-eyed and filled with adrenalin replied, "It was huge, Uncle Walter."

The fallen leaves in the southern hardwood forest were multicolored which, if Joseph had only wounded the deer, would make trying to find a blood trail to follow very difficult. The hunters searched for more than an hour. They crisscrossed the deer's trail and were about to give up when Walter spotted blood on a leaf. This discovery renewed their efforts.

Walter said, "I'll go back to the camp, pick up the beagle dogs and see if they can follow the trail." The oldest dog in the pack, Baby, picked up the trail immediately. She started barking and running and led Joseph straight to the deer. Woody and Walter had to hold him back to make him approach the deer with caution.

Baby ran straight to the deer's head, stopped, and barked in such a fashion as to tell Joseph to come claim his prize. The young hunter was so excited Woody could not hold him; he broke loose running as fast as he could, kicking leaves and jumping with joy. The deer was a beautiful ten pointer weighing two hundred eighty-seven pounds. Eventually the deer head was mounted and hung in the McKenzie's den.

Other lunch partners began to tell proud stories about their children and before many stories had been told the lunch hour was over. Woody enjoyed the hour and suggested that they meet frequently and have lunch together. It was a far cry from anything the former manager would have considered.

17

The office phone rang and Roberta answered. It was a woman's voice on the line. "I would like to talk to the person in charge of hiring. I'm not looking for a job myself but my husband used to work for OBM. Lawrance Wilson fired him and he would really like to come back to work for the company."

"Just a moment please." Roberta put the phone on hold. "I think you had better handle this one, Woody."

The caller explained that she wanted to get her husband reinstated. Sensing the need to talk privately with her, Woody asked if he could return her call. He wrote the number down, went to his office, and started to dial. Before he finished the seven digits, he decided not to use the office phone. He knew that the phone was still tapped and that the woman might have information that could be used by OBM.

He had to be careful not to let any usable information fall into the hands of Lawrance or any of his friends. Yet it was important to leave the phone taps in place so that some information could be purposefully leaked. It was a delicate balance.

He hung up the phone and immediately left the office headed for the pay phone he had used several times before. Jay Cee watched Woody leave and followed him. Woody wanted to signal him that everything was okay but there was no opportunity.

Woody stopped at the phone and, as on previous occasions, Jay Cee drove by and stopped at "the hill." Woody placed the call. The woman answered and explained how her husband had been fired. When she identified herself, Woody recalled the specifics that were involved. The story she told did not agree with Woody's recollection of the removal proceedings against her husband several months earlier.

"Would you and your husband mind coming by the complex to provide us with more details?"

"We would be glad to. Could we come by this afternoon? We would really like to get this cleared up as soon as possible."

"Yes, that will work out fine. Thanks for calling."

After their phone conversation ended, Woody returned to the office to prepare for the visitors. He wanted their story recorded, so he asked Roberta to sit in on the meeting to take notes.

Mrs. Samuel Thorn, the caller, arrived at the office with her husband about an hour later. As they entered the front door, it sounded like a family reunion was taking place. Everyone in the office gathered around the couple hugging, shaking hands, and asking how they were doing. It was obvious that the older couple had many friends at the company.

Woody was glad to see the warmth and

friendliness expressed by everyone toward the Thorns. He remembered Sam from times past, but had never met his wife. Roberta introduced them. Mrs. Thorn told Woody, "Sam spoke quite highly of you during the years he worked for OBM."

"I hope I can continue to earn Sam's respect. Would you come into my office so we can speak privately. Roberta, would you please wait outside for a few minutes while I explain what I want Mr. and Mrs. Thorn to do? Please have Bobbie Sue hold all calls."

If the couple agreed Roberta would join them and take notes of their conversation. The three stepped into Woody's office. "Would you have a seat on the sofa? How about a cup of coffee or coke?"

"No, nothing for us thanks. And we feel comfortable talking in front of Roberta."

He called Roberta in to take notes. "Just tell your story in your own words. Roberta will transcribe the notes and give you a copy. You can make changes or corrections as necessary."

As the couple began to tell their story,

Woody listened intently and Roberta wrote. He interrupted rarely and then only to clarify his understanding of the differences between what he had been told by Lawrance and what he was now hearing from Mr. Thorn.

Their story pointed out a huge problem that existed in OBM personnel policy whereby an unscrupulous manager such as Lawrance could totally abuse employees. There were not enough objective reviews in the disciplinary process to safeguard employees' rights.

It became increasingly evident that Mr. Thorn had been fired from OBM under false pretenses based on lies fabricated by Lawrance Wilson. After about an hour of discussion with the Thorns, Woody said, "I will do everything in my power to right this wrongful firing. What do you consider a fair settlement to be?"

"I want several things. First, I want my old job back. Second, I want back pay for the time I've been off. Third, I want you to present me with my thirty-five-year service pin. Fourth, I want to work one more day. Fifth, I want a retirement party honoring me for my long dedicated service to OBM, and finally, I want the local newspaper to cover my rehiring and retirement party."

"You can return to work tomorrow if you choose and I promise to seek approval of all of your other requests."

Mrs. Thorn began to cry tears of relief and joy. She and Sam were so delighted that Woody had taken time to listen to their story that emotion overcame both of them. Sam said, "I have a couple of carpentry jobs I'm working on, so I can't come to work tomorrow. I need about a week to complete those jobs. I want to report to work a week from next Monday."

"You can return to work when you want to and stay as long as you want." They agreed that a week from Monday would be a good time to return. How long he stayed could be decided later.

Woody assured Sam that things had changed at the complex. Roberta told them that the welcome they got when they entered the office today was an indication of how much the entire work force had missed him. They thanked

Roberta and Woody and left the office with joyful tears in their eyes.

"Roberta, will you transcribe the notes of the meeting as soon as possible? I want to send a copy to the Chairman with my recommendation that Sam's requests be approved with haste."

"I'll take care of it right away. I still want to continue my story, but I don't have time to finish it today. I don't want to start and stop again. I want to finish the whole story this time."

"I promise we will continue tomorrow."

Roberta left and began transcribing her notes. A superb typist, she was able to finish before her normal quitting time and gave Woody a copy of the transcribed notes. Woody had written a note to the Chairman and asked Roberta to fax all of it to him. She did then left for the day. Woody sat in his easy chair and felt good about the Thorn's situation.

As he reflected on the day's activities he wondered where all of these stories would lead. He was more embarrassed for OBM each time an employee talked about the treatment he/she received while under Lawrance's control. Each story was like a nail being driven into a coffin and the lid was being nailed tighter and tighter. How could one self-serving man damage OBM's long-standing reputation so greatly before being found out? Tighter controls, more inspections, or something must be done to prevent this from ever happening again. Maybe the answer was to make an example out of Lawrance and make sure that all other senior managers became intimately aware of actions he had taken and the results. Shaming him might prevent a situation like this from reoccurring. Woody gave the blind flashing signal to Jay Cee and once again they proceeded to the motel.

Woody didn't realize it but he was only seeing the tip of the iceberg.

18

The sun was just beginning to peek over the trees in the distance but it wasn't too early for a beagle to be making her customary morning rounds. The McKenzies had raised Baby from a sickly whining puppy to a muscular energetic example that any dog owner would be proud to claim. Her thick, shiny coat of ebony and brown was generously sprinkled with patches of white but what really set her apart were those soft brown, human-like eyes that were always filled with expression.

Naturally curious, a beagle seems to go through life investigating every moving object or any soft noise drifting faintly in the distance.

Baby spent many spring mornings, nose to the ground, at a dead run tracking the zig-zag path of rabbits. But squirrels and songbirds weren't safe from the natural hunter instinct either. From what appeared to be a sound sleep, Baby would suddenly raise her head, tilting it slightly to one side to better hear. Then, zeroing in on whatever noise had interrupted her slumber, would jump to all fours and be off at top speed. It was really not important to Baby if she caught the object of her harassment. The real pleasure was in the chase or in the knowledge that she was protecting her home turf.

Beagles seem to be gentle spirited animals and true to her breed Baby made a terrific pet. She could be called on in an instant to track a wounded deer during a hunt, and was just as comfortable stalking rabbits and quail with Woody and the boys. She was well-trained enough to stay back after scaring-up game but could be relied on to locate downed game.

Always leading Woody to the kill, Baby knew she would be praised highly for her deeds. And in the case of deer Woody rewarded her obedience by giving her a fresh piece of meat.

In an instant Baby could switch from seasoned hunting dog to docile yard pet and the McKenzie children and all of their friends took pleasure in her playful nature. As a watchdog Baby wasn't in perfect form, preferring to wag her tail and lick any stranger that might venture into the driveway rather than growl and bark. But she possessed a maternal instinct toward the kids as well as Woody and Martha that made her a fierce receptionist if they happened to be in the yard and unknown visitors arrived.

In short, Baby was a pleasure to own. She had truly become a member of the McKenzie family and was often the recipient of gifts from uneaten portions of school lunches or special treats brought home from town. Always willing to run and play with the kids or content to sun herself and sleep on warm days she was a key ingredient to the happiness of the family.

As the sun topped the trees Baby was concentrating on the elusive scent of rabbit through the open pasture next to the McKenzie back yard. Stopping, veering away from the path and losing the scent as the pungent aroma of wildflowers interrupted the animal's smell, Baby snorted to clear her nose. Picking up the scent again, the beagle was off at top speed nosing along the irregular path of the rabbit through the field.

Baby, on track and unbothered by the early morning songs of birds and the chattering of scurrying squirrels, ran down the gradual grade toward the edge of the woods. The smell was fresh and the dog quickened her pace anticipating the thrill of surprising her quarry. She could hear the gurgling of the branch as it meandered through the woods toward the larger creek and knew instinctively that the rabbit might be heading for a dense growth of briars that covered a freshly dug burrow along the bank. But, though the rabbit's fresh smell was all around the branch, the trail bypassed the brambles entirely.

What Baby did find was a turtle on a rock in the branch so she momentarily halted her quest to intimidate the scared reptile. A little frightened herself at the offensive smell of the turtle, Baby would bark and lunge at the hidden animal then jump back in fear.

This diversion lasted only a few moments before Baby again picked up the scent of the rabbit and remembered that she had been on the chase. She splashed across the cool water of the branch, stopping to lap up a quick drink before again running the trail. The rabbit had evidently run the branch for several yards and Baby negotiated the upper bank across exposed tree roots and fallen limbs, crouching under an occasional wild rose bush, never losing the smell of wild game.

The rabbit was a suitable adversary for the dog's abilities and had doubled back across the moving water in the direction of the pasture. Planning to circle around the beagle the rabbit had set a wandering, yet speedy course across the woods' edge. The open pasture lay only a few yards ahead and Baby knew she had a better chance of success not having to dodge undergrowth and jump logs. She was closing on the field and surely the rabbit when a sudden motion to her right caught her attention and she came to a sudden halt.

It wasn't just the motion that attracted the dog but also the smell. Saliva gathered in her mouth as her nose caught the scent of freshly cooked beef, a smell that said home and safety and security. Baby's tail began to wag. The smell of human was also flooding her senses but it was a human smell she didn't recognize. This confused her. She was used to the soothing smell of cooked meat being accompanied by the smells of the McKenzie family. She still interpreted the human smell as friendly and went up to the figure who was placing a large, juicy steak on the ground. She licked the meat at first then began to tear into it as the flavor delighted her senses.

"That's a good dog. Eat it up." Baby could feel the hands of the human vigorously rubbing her neck and she sat still, panting. The meat was so good after the tiring morning and a much more suitable reward than the stringy raw meat of a freshly killed rabbit. "Now let's go get some water, girl." She heard the slight click of metal but didn't realize that a leash had been attached to the ring on her collar until she moved toward the branch. At first it was merely a slight pressure at her neck but as the leash was pulled she realized she was forced into the direction of the pull.

After drinking enough water to soothe her throat from the meal, Baby gazed up at her captor and tried to understand what was going on. The smell of the leather leash was pleasant and she gnawed on it for a few seconds to test its strength. Its resistance felt good on her jaws but she realized she couldn't bite through.

Baby was led through the woods in the direction of the morning sun and the walk, at a brisk steady pace, felt good to her. Even though she couldn't identify her companion it was always good to be accompanied by a human on a morning stroll.

She could smell the faint odor of gasoline and oil several hundred yards before she actually spotted the truck parked along the edge of a gravel road. As the two exited the woods their path turned toward the pickup and their pace quickened slightly.

The truck had a topper with the door lifted open and the tailgate dropped making a large opening in the back of the pickup. Baby's companion led her into the back of the waiting truck. She lifted her nose at the strong smell of hay that filled the truck bed and saw the pile in the corner behind the cab. An old wool blanket covered the hay and as her companion closed the tailgate she trotted across to it. The truck bed was warm and after her busy morning, Baby was ready for a refreshing nap. As she nestled into the soft pile of hay she heard the loud slap of the topper door as it slammed shut behind her.

Soon the engine started. The fumes of gasoline grew stronger as the bed vibrated and the hum of the motor filled Baby's ears. The truck lurched forward and then sped up to an even speed. As the pickup moved along the curvy gravel road the beagle felt a sour taste and a nauseating feeling from the motion. She laid her head down to drift off to sleep.

The truck turned off the gravel road onto

the state highway and drove for several miles before turning onto another gravel road. The sound of the tires on the gravel woke the sleeping dog. She could see through the topper windows into the distance and saw cows grazing on a hillside. Nothing was familiar to Baby. She had been taken from her own territory into a totally unknown land.

At OBM's offices in Walnut hills Lawrance Wilson sat at his desk, doodling on his desk pad. He didn't like working here. He much preferred his territory at Bakersfield. Six feet tall, with a stocky athletic build, Lawrance walked with a confident swagger that let everyone know he was in control. His dark hair and smooth olive complexion were instant attractions to most women. He took an evil sort of pleasure in using his good looks and practiced charm to seduce whomever could meet his needs at the moment. When asked why he wore his hair longer than most, he would pull a lock to the side and reply, "This hair gives me extraordinary power over women. They love to run their fingers through it. It's like a magnet, they become aroused just by touching it." Lawrance had a sixth sense that told him when people were at their most vulnerable, and he frequently managed to work that angle to his advantage.

Lawrance didn't hear his office door open so he didn't look up when the figure silently entered the room. He walked across the soft carpet and settled into an overstuffed chair across from Lawrance. Lawrance caught the movement from the corner of his eye and he looked up startled. "Oh, it's you. Well?"

"I brought you a present." He tossed a package on Lawrance's desk tied in plain brown paper. Lawrance tore through the paper and opened the box. A smile slowly formed on his face. In the bottom, in tissue paper was a dog collar. On it was a tag embossed:

Baby

Woody McKenzie

Walnut Hills, Mississippi

19

Jay Cee came to Woody's room and they chatted for a while. Not only was he an excellent bodyguard, he was also a superb listener and pretty good amateur psychologist. He helped Woody turn loose of some of the day's anxieties and tensions. Woody asked his friend if any supper surprises were in store for today. He replied, "You never know, take a shower and we'll see."

Woody took a nice long soothing, hot shower. He stepped out of the shower, wrapped a towel around his waist, entered the room, and sat on his bed. On the night stand near his bed was a glass of red wine. Woody, remembering a consultation with his doctor that a glass of wine each day was good for the body and soul, sat on the side of the bed and very slowly and deliberately moved the glass under his nose to smell the bouquet. He took a sip and rolled it around in his mouth tingling his taste buds. It was wonderful and Woody could not play with the wine any longer. He took a couple of gulps and the glass was empty.

As he sat on the bed feeling the warm liquid flow down his throat to his stomach, his whole body became very warm and relaxed. He slid around in the bed closing his eyes as he gently laid down. He drifted into a soft sleep for thirty to forty-five minutes.

He was awakened by the television as it changed programs. It sounded like someone had increased the volume but it was just one program going off and another coming on. A commercial was blasting with an automobile salesman screaming about "The last sale of the century. There will never be another one like this one."

Woody got up, put his clothes on and walked to the restaurant. He had no idea where Jay Cee was, and as he had been told, went about his business. He knew Jay Cee was close at hand but his friend was nowhere to be seen in the restaurant. Woody had recently been diagnosed with high cholesterol and as usual he searched the menu for low cholesterol or cholesterol-free selections. Pictures of a couple of good looking items caught his eye — baked fish and smoked chicken.

Woody remembered his early childhood days when baked fish was unheard of. If you didn't fry fish at Trey and Ethel's home, you didn't eat fish. Woody recalled the many times, especially during the spring, when he and his dad put their nets in the Sunflower River. One occasion permanently etched in his memory was the time they put the hoop nets out near a dense thicket of willow trees. His dad said, "We should catch a boat-full of channel cats here."

After the nets had been in the river for three days, it was time to check them and see if Trey's prediction had come true. The boat they used was small, about ten feet long with side boards not more than eight inches high, light and easy to move around with the short, wooden paddles Trey made. Since they stayed close to the willow grove there was less river current working against them.

As they approached the net location with caution, Trey threw the grapple hook out, let it sink to the bottom, and began to reel in. He knew exactly where to throw to hook the net the first time. He began to pull on the line and said, "I feel the net shaking." As his big arms flexed their muscles and the net came closer to the surface, Woody saw the grapple cord tighten and quiver. He knew they had a big catch as the net hoops began to break the surface and the water rolled. The net was loaded with channel catfish. Young Woody got more and more excited as the net rose out of the water. Finally he was able to get his hands on the net and hold it until his Dad could release the grapple hook.

Carefully father and son worked together pulling the net into the boat. Woody could not believe his eyes and began to shout with joy. His Dad told him to hush. "Don't make so much noise. We don't want the neighbors to know where our net is." When all the fish were shaken out of the net, eighty-two "head" filled the little boat.

"We have four hundred pounds of fish in this boat," Trey said. It was about to sink so they carefully reset the net and headed through the willow thicket to the bank. Ethel had heard Woody's screaming and walked down to the river to see what all the commotion was about. She likewise was amazed at the fish they had caught in the one net.

Woody snapped back to the present, looking around the restaurant hoping to see Jay Cee and tell him about this childhood flashback. They had fished many times with Trey and he knew his friend would remember this fish story. Not seeing him, Woody ordered supper thinking how much fun it would be to remember this story with his old friend. He stored the memory away and at the next opportunity intended to reminisce with Jay Cee about those carefree days. Woody finished his meal and returned to his room.

20

Woody didn't see Jay Cee until the next morning as they headed to the complex. He remembered his promise to Roberta and wondered what he could do to make her burden lighter. He went to the office and began work on the ever-increasing mountain of paperwork. There were bills to pay and some were getting old. He had asked Bobbie Sue to arrange them in priority with the ones that needed the most immediate attention on top. The organization had a strict prompt payment policy. Each person was expected to do their part to ensure that payments were made in accordance with the policy. Woody worked feverishly on the stack and by noon had made considerable progress. He wanted to shift gears after lunch and continue with the employee interviews.

Woody asked Roberta to make arrangements with Tommy for the first employee to be available at 1:00 p.m. Little did he know, however, that another dark cloud from the headquarters office was about to descend on the complex. The Chairman had told him that two auditors would be coming to look at procurement procedures. He didn't expect them to be two females, one white whose name was Frances and the other black named Debra. Not only were they auditors in common, they also shared the same last name. Woody also did not expect them to be so thorough and precise. Woody had gone through audits before and generally it was just a "going through the motions drill." Not so this time.

They arrived unannounced. Woody would find out later that is the way "headhunting audits" are performed. Given the situation at the complex that is exactly the way the Chairman wanted this audit conducted. The Chairman told Woody later that he did not want the office employees who might be loyal to the "other side" to be forewarned. As it turned out all of the office force were loyal to OBM and had objected strongly to action taken previously by Lawrance.

The auditors began to inspect the cabinets crammed with transaction records. They required that all files be secured and locked so that no one would have the opportunity to tamper with them and the locks were replaced with their own set. That way anyone needing to get to the files would have to do so under the watchful eye of one of the auditors. Woody was amazed that such precautions were being taken and asked Frances, "Why?"

"It looks like some big time fraud has been going on around here and it's our job to secure enough documentation to be able to press criminal charges. We have to stay detached from the people here until we find out exactly what has been going on and who all is involved."

"Well, I thought we were all on the same team and I hope you find what you're looking for. Is there anything you need from me? Office space? Keys? Anything?"

"Thanks, but we are completely self-sufficient. We'll let you know if we need anything. And most of our research will be done during normal office hours."

Woody thought, "Wow! How could such a nice-looking person be so cold and professional?" He would find out later in life after she took her "auditor's glasses" off, that she was a warm, gentle, caring person.

Frances turned to Debra and said, "Well, we need to get to work." They exited Woody's office and started the arduous process of reviewing every procurement action that had taken place in the last five years.

Woody asked Roberta to send in the next interviewee. He listened to detailed stories about painting buildings outside the complex and pouring concrete at locations fifteen to twenty miles away from OBM property. All the employees believed they were correct in their actions because Lawrance had directed them to do the jobs. Little did they know that they were lining the malicious manager's pockets at their expense and the expense of OBM.

Likewise, little did they know that someone was photographing them and making a detailed record of their activities. This secret photographer, known as "The Kid", had always been suspicious of Lawrance and his use of company personnel. As a result of training he had received in the U.S. Marine Corps, he was alert and recognized the many situations that appeared to be inappropriate use of materials, supplies, and manpower.

Tim, "The Kid", had applied for employment at OBM several times before he was eventually hired. Each time a job vacancy that he considered himself qualified to fill was announced, he submitted the written forms and participated in oral interviews. Two times he left the interview feeling he was the best qualified applicant. Each time he was disappointed with the reason given for not being hired, that his paperwork was not complete or was not received before the cut-off date.

Upon receiving notice that he would not

be hired after his third interview, Tim asked the personnel officer, "Will you please review my application with me? I want to know what I'm doing wrong."

"Sure, I'll be glad to review your application, but the fact is you didn't submit an application."

"That's absurd. I certainly did. I mailed it to Lawrance's office two days after the vacancy notice appeared in the local newspaper."

"Well there is not one in your official folder so I can only assume you didn't submit one."

Tim's face reddened as his anger mounted at the realization that Lawrance had not forwarded his application to the personnel officer. He said, "Thank you, sir, I understand what is happening to my applications. The next one will be sent to you by certified mail."

"That will be fine and I can assure you I will review it and consider you for appointment assuming you are qualified."

The Kid was hired a month later much to Lawrance's chagrin. It didn't take long for the wisdom of that selection to come into question. From the time he was hired by OBM, Lawrance made every effort to give him the most difficult and demeaning tasks. Lawrance frequently took job assignment duties related to Tim away from the foreman and made sure that the most rancid, contaminated jobs were assigned to him. Tim well remembered those dirty assignments and took considerable pleasure and satisfaction in the secret pictures he was taking and the particulars associated with Lawrance's actions. His records and photographs would play a major role in the investigation.

About 4:30 Roberta said, "It's my turn again." She came into Woody's office and closed the door saying, "Since all the office employees are gone, I feel more comfortable with the door closed." She told Woody once again that Lawrance had used his immense power of persuasion on her. She had fallen completely for his line, "If you are loyal to me, I'll take care of you. I'll give you awards, I'll promote you — just believe in me." In the beginning she was a dedicated employee who believed Lawrance could do no wrong.

"My belief in him began to crumble when he constantly asked me to come to his office to take dictation. He always insisted that we sit side-by-side on the sofa even after I explained that it was hard to take dictation that way and I preferred to sit at the conference table." Lawrance agreed, but as they completed each memo he would ask her to sit on the sofa and read it out loud. The memos were short, meaningless, shallow, and without any coherent thoughts. They did not request anything or answer anything and were nothing more than a string of loose sentences.

After Roberta read the memos, Lawrance always wanted to sit with her and daydream for a while, not allowing her to leave the room until he had given her an affectionate peck on the cheek. She thought, "This is strange." This activity went on a couple of times a day for about a month. Roberta's other work began to pile up and she asked Lawrance if someone else could take the dictation.

"Absolutely not. You're the senior administrative person and I'm the senior supervisor so we have to work together. Get your coat on, we need to go on a field trip."

Since it was 3 o'clock and she was only supposed to work until 4, she said, "I hope it's a short trip." As they went outside and drove off, he told her they would be back before quitting time.

When OBM bought the property and constructed the Bakersfield complex, a deal was made by the acquisition team to purchase all of the property owned by the same estate. Sort of "I'll sell you what you want, but only if you agree to buy all I want to sell." As a result the estate owner's home was also purchased and was now owned and maintained by OBM for company use. Lawrance drove to one of the houses and told Roberta to get out. As they entered, he told her he wanted to renovate it and needed her opinion on bedroom colors.

"The girls in the office told me you have an eye for color. Judging from the bright colors you wear to work, I would have to say that is an understatement. Your clothes look great and really turn me on."

Roberta blushed, "Thanks for the compliment I'm flattered you noticed."

To Roberta's amazement the house was in good condition. It had been freshly painted and new furniture installed. Lawrance preceded her down the hall toward a back bedroom, opened the door and asked her to come in. After looking around for a few minutes Lawrance flopped down on the bed. "These springs feel pretty good. Why don't you sit on the side and give me your thoughts?"

The box springs began to creak as she carefully let her body rest on the bed. Lawrance said, "Go ahead, lie down and see what you think."

Thoughtfully, she swung her feet on the bed and stretched out. She stayed there about thirty seconds and starting to get up said, "They seem fine to me."

He grabbed her by the arm and said, "Let's give the springs the real test."

"No thank you," As she got up and walked down the hall he followed.

"You might as well let me have some. When you go back to the office they will know you've been to 'the house.' No one comes to this house and leaves without being screwed."

"I'll tell Jacqueline that even though I came to this house I didn't put out." She went outside, got in the car, and waited for Lawrance to join her.

A few minutes later he came out and they drove back to the complex. Neither one said a word. As they entered the security gates they saw three female office workers looking out the window toward them. Roberta was the first to get out of the car and enter the office. She called all of them into her office, explained in detail what had happened and what had not happened. She reminded them that they were junior employees to her and that she had better not hear any comments made about what they thought happened. Any explaining that needed to be done would be done by her. She did not want any vicious rumors started that could get back to her husband. Their relationship was fragile already and could not stand any more stress and strain.

"All of you know John gets drunk every weekend and beats me when he comes home. He does that as a matter of routine just to me show how strong he is. If he ever suspected that I was having an affair he would kill me."

For the next few weeks working relationships were strained and Lawrance did not ask her to take any dictation. It seemed like Lawrance was turning his office affection back to Jacqueline Brick once again. About six weeks after the house incident, Lawrance called Roberta into his office. "Here's the key to the house, I need you to go check it out, make sure it's clean and well-stocked with food. Some big shots are coming from the home office and I want everything ready when they get here."

"Okay, it should only take me about an hour." Although Roberta had some apprehensions about returning to the house she felt safe knowing she could lock the doors behind her. Thinking she had the only set of keys, she went in and locked both locks from the inside.

She had been there ten or fifteen minutes when a car drove up. She looked out the window and saw Lawrance getting out and heading for the door. Her heart raced as he knocked on the door, "Roberta, unlock the door."

"I'll be out in just a minute," Roberta carefully eased her way though the house toward the back door. Her plan was to go out and give him the keys. She quietly unlocked both locks and gently pulled on the door. It wouldn't budge. She shook it harder. Roberta realized that a security bar was preventing the door from opening. At this point, still trying to stay calm, she decided to slip out one of the back windows. Again she walked very quietly down the hall to the back bedroom. She pulled the curtain open and discovered security screening on the window. As her heart raced out of control, she realized that she was trapped and began to panic. She kept saying to herself, "Don't panic; calm down."

"What's the hold up?"

"I can't come just yet, hold on."

Lawrance, knowing that he had her trapped decided to use his keys to open the door.

Roberta was standing by the door when she heard him turn his key in the lock. She ran to the back bedroom, locked the door, and grabbed the phone to call someone — anyone, but there was no dial tone. The phone was dead. By this time Lawrance was in the house and had secured both locks again. He called to her. She did not answer. She could hear him looking in each room as he worked his way down the hall. When he got to the back bedroom he tried to turn the door knob. He realized then that she had locked herself in the bedroom. To Lawrance this was part of a "kinky game" she wanted to play.

"Roberta..."

She did not answer.

"I know you're in there and I have something you're going to enjoy. All you have to do is open the door and we can have some fun."

She was terrified.

He continued to tap lightly on the door.

She was paralyzed with fear.

Suddenly, he kicked the door in and saw Roberta standing in the corner farthest from the door. He walked toward her slowly as she pleaded with him to let her go, "Don't do this to me."

"You don't need to go. You're just playing a game with me. I know you want to screw me." He moved closer.

"Please let me leave. I'll quit my job and never come back to the complex again."

"I don't want you to leave this house or the complex until I've had you."

By this time he was close enough to touch her arm. She couldn't breathe. He gently rubbed her exposed arm. "You have beautiful red hair. I bet you're red all over." He moved closer, gently rubbing more of her exposed arm and touching her neck. As a result of his slow gentle approach she became less rigid and breathed easier. He moved closer so that he was standing directly in front of her and continued to slide his hands down her curvaceous body and waist. "You are so beautiful and I've wanted you for too long," he kissed her on the side of her face and neck. The hot breath on her neck was driving her crazy.

"Don't do this to me."

She had become almost totally limp. He put his arms around her, pulled her close, and kissed her lips passionately. Her skin was hot and stimulated. He licked her lips and slipped his tongue into her mouth. She was becoming more excited as he unbuttoned her blouse and caressed her breasts. He pulled her skirt up and began to caress her thighs. His hands moved higher and higher until they were in her panties. At that point she leaned her head on his shoulder and began to whimper. He grabbed her, laid her on the bed and continued to undress her. She was caught in his spell. In just a few minutes they were both completely undressed.

Roberta hesitated in her story, turned to Woody and said, "I know you think I'm a weak person, maybe an easy mark. I just didn't know what to do."

Woody didn't know what to say or do. He was dumbfounded at the graphic detail Roberta used to describe her encounter.

"We stayed in bed for the rest of the day and into the night. I forgot all about time, almost like I had been drugged. We must have drifted off to sleep because about 10:00 a car pulled into the driveway and somebody came to the door. Lawrance was asleep so I looked out the window and saw the deputy sheriff's car. By the time I got back to the bedroom, Lawrance was up jerking on his pants. That's when the deputy radioed that he had found my car."

Roberta's husband, John, was at the sheriff's office and heard the call come in. He ran out of the office, jumped in his car, and headed toward the house. Lawrance had opened the door and stepped out. The deputy met him and said, "You better get out of here, her husband's on the way and you don't want to run into him." Lawrance went back into the house, grabbed his keys, ran outside, jumped in his car, and left.

He was five miles down the road before he realized that he did not have a shirt or shoes on. He began to wonder how he was going to explain this to his wife. Although it was not unusual for him to come home late, it would be difficult to explain coming home half naked.

Now it was Lawrance's turn to panic. What could he say that would present a plausible explanation to his wife? He had not anticipated his afternoon with Roberta would leave them both exhausted. He certainly had not anticipated that he would fall asleep. He planned to have a "quickie" and leave. Now, however, much to his chagrin, his sexual prowess had presented a huge problem.

Looking down the road Lawrance saw an approaching car. As the two cars met he recognized it as the one belonging to Roberta's husband, John. It was apparent that John also recognized Lawrance's car. The enraged husband slammed on his brakes, slid to a stop, and immediately turned the car around as Lawrance watched in his rearview mirror. Recognizing that he was facing a madman if he were caught, Lawrance stomped the accelerator as the other car gave chase. Lawrance had a one-half to three-quarter mile lead on the car and soon reached a crossroad where he had to make a calculated move. Rather than turning toward the complex he turned in the opposite direction toward town. With his headlights off, he sped away. In a minute or so Lawrance saw John stop at the crossroad to determine his move. He turned toward the complex. Seeing what had happened, Lawrance breathed a sigh of relief and continued to drive with his lights off until the tail lights in his rearview mirror disappeared. Lawrance turned his lights on and sped away.

He still had a problem though: no shoes and no shirt.

He asked himself, "How am I going to explain this to Juanita?" Although he had clothes at the complex he knew Roberta's husband might be there. He ruled out going there and began to develop a bizarre story to cover his tracks. He decided to siphon gas out of the car and sprinkle just enough on his pants to leave a strong scent. He would tell the story that he had car trouble and gas had spilled on him. After spilling the gas on his clothes, he crawled into the road ditch and rolled in the mud and water. He got back in the car to drive home.

As he pulled into the driveway, he honked

the car horn. He wanted Juanita to feel sorry for him and help him inside. When she heard the horn blowing, Lawrance's wife opened the front door and came out. He stopped the car and called for her to come help. She ran to the car and asked what in the world had happened. He said there was a problem with the car and gas had spilled on his clothes. The gas fumes were so strong he had to throw his shoes and shirt away. Juanita called the kids to come outside and help their daddy. She ran inside, turned the shower on, and helped Lawrance take his pants off and step in the shower. Lawrance had forgotten that he did not have any underclothes on. He would take a shower and have time to develop a story to cover that small but rather significant detail.

By this time Roberta's husband had gone to the house where the deputy had found her car. She and the deputy were there and had agreed on what they would say about the situation. They told her husband that her car would not start and since the phone at the house didn't work she had no way to call for help. A conspiracy was in the making. By the time John arrived they had the hood up and she was sitting in the driver's seat ready to crank it. As he turned in the driveway she cranked the motor and pressed the accelerator to the floor. This was supposed to give credence to the story they would tell. John jumped out and began screaming at his wife, "Where the hell have you been? I've look all over the county for you and then sat at the police station for two hours."

"I had to come out here to check out the house. Can I help it if the car won't start? I've been telling you something is wrong with it."

"Sure, have you ever heard of a telephone? I know you were out here to meet somebody."

"Look, go in there and try the phone, it won't work either. And who in the world would I meet out here? I'd still be stuck if Ed here hadn't found me. You couldn't have looked very hard or you would have been here." She said the deputy did something under the hood that allowed the car to crank.

"Now John, just calm down. There's no

harm done, the automatic choke got stuck and flooded the engine but I got it unstuck with a screwdriver."

"Stay out of this Ed. It's none of your business. Just how long has Lawrance Wilson been gone?"

"Don't be ridiculous John, Lawrance hasn't been here, I haven't seen him since I left the office at 3:00."

John was extremely jealous and suspected that Roberta was having an affair with every man in the county. Lawrance's well-known reputation as a womanizer made him particularly suspect. Roberta knew how hot-headed and irrational John was. He always carried a pistol and rifle with him. She knew that if he and Lawrance had met on the road, John would have taken a shot at Lawrance. He was an extremely possessive person and had told her he would kill the son-of-a-bitch if he ever caught them together.

Roberta was not out of the woods yet, but she was relieved somewhat that John had not stopped Lawrance. She hoped the deputy's story was convincing enough. After John calmed down, he and Roberta headed home. When they pulled in the driveway he jumped out of the car and ran up to Roberta just as she opened her car door. He reached in, grabbed a hand full of red hair, snatched her out, and slammed her head against the side of the car breaking her nose.

She pleaded, "Please don't hit me anymore," and raised her hands to shield against his attack. With blood gushing from her nose, she stumbled toward the house.

John yelled, "I'll kill you. I know you've been sleeping with Lawrance. I'll hunt him down and shoot him like a wild dog."

The blood blurred her vision as she staggered toward the doorsteps. John grabbed her arm and threw her to the ground saying, "You'll not get in this house alive. I'll break every bone in your body."

Yelling for help as she crawled toward the door, Roberta pleaded, "Don't hurt me anymore."

Their two sons were standing in the door witnessing the horrible beating Roberta was taking. Twelve-year old Jason could not watch any longer and ran toward his father. Although the boy weighed one-hundred pounds less than his father, when they collided both fell down. By this time a neighbor had arrived and helped Roberta to her feet and inside. He said, "I've called the sheriff's office and 911. They should be here any minute."

"Please help Jason. John will hurt him too.

He turned to David, the younger son, and said, "Get your mother a wet towel. I'll go help Jason." As he ran outside two other neighbors arrived and were holding John face down on the ground. The deputy pulled in with lights flashing, the ambulance following close behind.

The deputy, Ed Dolan, yelled, "Hold John, I'm coming with the handcuffs."

John, kicking and swearing said, "Ed, if you put those cuffs on me, I'll kill you."

"John, the best thing you can do is shut up and come with me. Don't make your situation worse by resisting arrest. You can calm down in jail tonight and tomorrow we'll let the judge decide what needs to happen."

"You can't take me to jail. I want to see a lawyer."

"You have the right to remain silent. If you choose not to, anything you say can and will be used against you in a court of law. Do you understand?"

"Yeah, I understand. I'll get you for this, Ed. Maybe you want to lock me up so you can come see Roberta too."

"That's enough. Shut up and get in the car."

The ambulance rushed Roberta to the hospital emergency room. The sheriff came by, picked up the two kids and took them home to spend the night with his family. Roberta remained in the hospital overnight and was released late the next day. She immediately signed peace bond papers against John and began divorce proceedings. She was able to return to work in a few of days.

Roberta had been talking to Woody relating her story for about two hours without interruption. Woody was so engrossed in her story he lost track of time. He looked out the office window and there sat Jay Cee peering directly toward him from across the large parking lot. Woody told Roberta that they had to leave the office. If necessary they could continue her story later.

"Okay, and yes there is more to tell."

21

Woody got very little sleep that night. He answered the wake-up call at 5:30 as usual but this time rather than getting up, he rolled over and went back to sleep.

Jay Cee was up and out making his rounds. At 6:00 a.m., he returned to his room to shower and quickly realized something must be wrong because he did not hear Woody next door. He very carefully opened the connecting room doors and found Woody still in bed. Jay Cee was frightened; however, his CIA training prevailed. Rather than enter the room, he drew his service revolver and called to Woody in a low voice. When he got no response, he called again in a little louder voice. This time Woody answered and said, "I'm okay, I'm getting up."

Jay Cee was standing beside the connecting doors with his service revolver in the ready position still not convinced that everything was okay. His thoughts were racing and questioning. Had someone entered his friend's room that night? Was someone hiding in the room waiting for Jay Cee to enter?

This time he called to Woody and told him to get up and come to his room. When Woody walked through the door opening, Jay Cee grabbed him and slammed the door.

Startled and barely awake, Woody asked, "What's this all about? Why are you acting like this? I just didn't want to get up and go to work today."

"Unless you're sick enough to go to the hospital you will go to work."

"I'm so tired of the whole mess, I'm ready to leave and drop the investigation."

"You can't do that. Too many people have already stepped forward and if the investigation ended here those honest people would be destroyed." Jay Cee told him the mission was crucial and he had to continue. Woody knew Jay Cee was right and returned to his room to shower.

Realizing that Woody was thirty to forty-five minutes behind schedule, Jay Cee went to the restaurant and got pancakes, coffee, and orange juice. By the time Woody had finished dressing, Jay Cee had returned with his breakfast. Woody was amazed with the ease Jay Cee could move around and never be seen. "How do you do it?"

"Tricks of the trade. You learn to blend in and constantly change your outward appearance." He told Woody some days his outward appearance changed so much he could pass as a "white dude." Woody just shook his head and thanked Jay Cee for getting him up and also for the reminder that a lot of people were depending on him.

Once Woody arrived at the complex, he realized that Jay Cee was right. As the day progressed he was able to find renewal in the routine of the daily grind. As the day drew to a close Roberta knocked on Woody's door.

"Woody, the other subject I want to talk about is John's death. Everyone in the community thought John died of a drug overdose, but that was not what really happened. He was murdered about six months after his release from jail. Lawrance had blackmailed me into having sex with Ed Dolan by threatening to tell John about our affair. He knew John was insanely jealous and finding out I was sleeping with another man would have triggered his rage beyond control. I was snared in another trap set by Lawrance with no way out."

"Did you consider reporting this to the sheriff? Surely he would have put a stop to any abuse you were suffering at the hand of his deputy."

"No, Woody, you don't understand the conspiracy between Lawrance and the local law enforcement officers. The sheriff would have laughed me out of his office and then told Lawrance. That would have made my situation with Lawrance turn from psychological and sexual abuse to physical abuse as well. John had beaten me so many times I just couldn't stand any more. One day when Lawrance and I were at the house, John caught us. He tried to kick the door in, but had no luck. He ran around the house waving a shotgun and shouting for us to come outside. Lawrance called Ed on the car phone and told him to come to the house immediately. John was so frustrated he rammed the front door with the pickup truck. He rammed the door so hard the second time it crashed in and he flew into the windshield, knocking himself out. At that moment Ed drove up and jumped out with his pistol drawn. He could see John slumped over the steering wheel with blood streaming from his head.

"Ed moved closer to John and realized that he was unconscious. He called to Lawrance to come out because they had a mess on their hands. Lawrance pushed his way through the opening beside the truck, telling Ed it looked like he had it under control and for him to take care of John for good. He told Ed if he ever wanted to enjoy my company again he would have to get rid of John permanently."

"I joined them and asked if they were

going to let John bleed to death. I wanted to get him out of the truck and stop the bleeding. They wouldn't let me touch him. Ed got out a syringe and I started screaming. Lawrance held me while Ed injected John with something into his neck. I kicked as hard as I could but Lawrance pulled me back into the house. There was nothing I could do."

Woody was silent for a few moments. "Wasn't there an autopsy and an investigation into his death?"

"No. Lawrance and the local law officers took care of the situation and John was buried without any questions being asked."

Woody looked out the window and sighed.

22

Woody drove to the complex arriving about an hour late and went directly to his office. He was behind on his interview schedule. Needing to get away from Roberta's story for a while, he asked her who should be interviewed next. The Chairman wanted all interviews completed not later than the end of the following week. At the rate Woody was going, it might take all month. Hopefully other interviews would not last as long as Roberta's.

Much to Woody's surprise, Roberta had selected The Kid next. "Why did you put him ahead of the other senior personnel who have worked at the complex for twenty or more years?"

"The Kid is a photographic genius; he

has a detailed collection of pictures that can be used against Lawrance."

"He should provide that type of information to Doc Holmes. All I want to do is reconcile the differences between employee contracts and the duties they were actually performing."

"I really think you should talk to him even if it's only for ten minutes."

"Okay, can you have him here in two hours?"

"No need to wait that long, he's already here."

"How did you know I would agree to interview him?"

Roberta just smiled as she ushered The Kid in. He came in and gave Woody a strong, firm handshake. He was extremely courteous and thanked Woody for the opportunity to tell his story. He seemed a bit nervous and it reminded Woody of his own nervousness a while back in the Chairman's office. Woody wanted to make The Kid comfortable and asked him if he wanted coffee, coke, or anything to drink.

"No sir. I don't want to waste any of your

valuable time."

"I appreciate that. Let's get started." Woody told him to start wherever he wanted to and tell anything he thought would be helpful to OBM.

The Kid reached in his coat pocket and pulled out a photo album containing twenty, or so, black and white prints. He had a written narrative that accompanied each photograph. The narratives identified the people in the pictures, locations, times of day, and dates they were taken.

Woody was fascinated with the information he was seeing and asked, "Do you have other copies stored somewhere?"

The Kid leaned back in his chair, broke into a big grin, and said, "Yes sir. Copies are locked away in three different safety deposit boxes in three different towns."

"Why did you spend so much time photographing Lawrance?"

"I'm a Marine veteran, and I worked at the complex before Lawrance became manager although I was not working here at the time he moved to the manager's position. Each time I submitted an application, Lawrance would refuse to forward it to the personnel office to rehire me." The Kid knew he had certain rights which were being violated and he had confronted Lawrance on several occasions. Every time Lawrance acted like a "real ass."

"I knew about Lawrance's womanizing reputation and thought it would be helpful to my future employment opportunities if I could catch Lawrance and some of his teen-aged baby-sitters in compromising situations. I followed him one night and got a big break. Lawrance and Juanita had attended a social function and got home about midnight. Juanita went into the house, the baby-sitter came out and got in the car with Lawrance to go home. I had my night-vision glasses with me and I could see everything that was going on. When Lawrance turned around and left the driveway, I was right behind him."

"Lawrance was too engrossed with the young girl to realize that he was being tailed. He drove to a secluded spot about two miles from his house. Then he opened both front doors and stripped down as the girl also took off her clothes. She was the daughter of one of the local big shots and had the reputation of being a foxy, hot chick. I was watching the action through my night vision glasses. I let them get involved. Her legs were spread wide open and sticking straight up in the air. Lawrance fell down on top of her. I moved close enough that I could hear them moaning and groaning. I crept to one side and with my camera focused on the couple, called to Lawrance. When he turned his head, I snapped the picture. As the flash went off, Lawrance yelled.

"I ran to my truck and left the scene fully convinced I could play hardball with Lawrance. I thought my unemployment problems were over."

The Kid continued to follow Lawrance and photograph him along with OBM's employees working at locations unrelated to and far removed from the complex.

Woody understood why Roberta was so interested in The Kid telling his story. "Do you want to tell any more?"

"Just one more example should do the trick. This time Lawrance and his current girlfriend were parked near a church about two miles from the complex. The church had been there for over one hundred years and, as most old churches, had a cemetery behind it. This time Lawrance's vehicle got stuck. When I sneaked up to the car and snapped the picture, Lawrance lost his sense of direction. Rather than back out of the church's parking lot, he went forward and turned behind the church. It had rained for several days and the ground was soaked. In order to miss a big oak tree and turn, Lawrance slowed down. The car began to sink. Lawrance pressed the accelerator harder, the car lunged forward and all four wheels sank into the soggy ground. He tried to rock the car forward and backward to get it moving. Each time he changed direction the car sank deeper. All four wheels were mired up in two different graves. I was watching all of this, taking pictures, and laughing hysterically. Lawrance jumped out and told the girl to drive forward.

He was behind pushing and mud was flying from under each wheel. Lawrance was being plastered and yelled at the girl to stop. It was plain that the car would have to be towed from the cemetery.

"I took several more photographs and left. The next day I went back to the church and photographed the deep ruts in the cemetery. The church leaders were upset and trying to determine who had desecrated the cemetery. It wasn't hard to find the culprit, especially since the pastor got an anonymous phone call telling him which tow truck had removed the vehicle."

"Thanks for giving me the opportunity to tell my story."

"Take some time to put your thoughts together and be prepared to withstand a cross examination by Doc Holmes. You have photographic evidence that will substantiate claims by other employees. I'll recommend to Doc that you be interviewed first and remain available for recall. The information you provide will be sworn testimony and will be useful to pry statements from other less cooperative employees."

The Kid seemed eager to cooperate and pledged his full support. Woody told him that his veteran status would assure him of a permanent position in OBM. Once again The Kid thanked Woody for his time.

Woody called Roberta to his office. She walked in with a smug, proud look on her face knowing she had struck a death blow to Lawrance.

"Do you have any more bombshells to drop, Roberta?"

Looking pleased with herself, she said, "I might!"

Woody was not surprised with her self-satisfaction. Now she was in a position to deal some misery to Lawrance like he had dealt her. This woman's scorn was coming out and she was enjoying every minute of it. He sensed a killer instinct in Roberta. She was becoming very deliberate and focused. The look in her eyes reflected the intensity in her speech. She was on a mission and would "cross every t and dot every i" to ensure completion to her satisfaction. Woody had not seen anyone so intent since his discussion with the Chairman at the start of this action.

She was ready to dig in and go after Lawrance. Her intensity caused Woody some concern. He said, "You can't use OBM's action against Lawrance as a vehicle to satisfy your personal vendetta."

"No problem, for the first time in three years, I have hope."

23

Woody sat back in his leather chair. He made a three hundred-sixty degree turn, slowly looking at the room, how it was decorated and all of the furnishings. Photographs hanging on the wall depicted scenes from the early years of operation. The conference table was made of red oak and had a beautiful finish and shine on it. The chairs were upholstered in navy blue with intricate designs in the material. The sofa was brown leather and matched his desk chair. They were both very comfortable to sit in. His desk matched the conference table. As he looked around the room, he wondered how anyone could act as irresponsibly as Lawrance had. What would possess anyone to act in such a manner as to jeopardize his position with this organization?

The background Woody experienced as a child made him appreciate his position with OBM. Throughout his career, he had made a good living for himself and his family. He realized he would never get rich, but at the same time he knew that his family had much more than many of his friends. He believed Lawrance had always had plenty and was a spoiled child who had grown up without any genuine dreams.

Many times Woody reflected on his own early childhood and appreciated the valuable lessons he had learned. By some standards, it was a childhood without much more than the basics of life, some would say underprivileged. Woody would say they were wrong. He said many times that he was privileged to have seen those with more than he, for they gave him a sense of direction. He wanted those same things and now that he had them, he appreciated them much more than those who had nice things all their lives.

Woody shook his head, snapping himself out of the daydream he was enjoying. He had work to do — people to interview. Roberta's enthusiasm had rubbed off on him. He called Bobbie Sue on the intercom and asked her to go to the local bakery and pick up a cake large enough for the office staff, and also some chocolate and vanilla ice cream.

"What is going on?" she asked.

"I feel like celebrating and I'd like to share some time with others in the office."

"Yes sir."

Woody handed her twenty dollars, gave her the keys to his car, and said go spend it on refreshments. She grabbed her purse and headed to the parking lot.

In his excitement Woody had forgotten that Jay Cee was sitting in the parking lot across the road. He didn't know how to signal that everything was okay. He knew his friend would see his car leave with Bobbie Sue driving and would wonder what was going on. Woody quickly closed the blinds just as if he were leaving the office. He walked to the main entrance of the building and went outside. Although he could not see Jay Cee, he felt sure Jay Cee could see him. Seeing the car leave, the blinds closed, and Woody standing on the front balcony would be cause for concern. Woody, realizing he needed to give the okay signal, walked around on the porch, stretching his arms and legs as if he were taking a break from his work. He walked back and forth on the porch soaking up the fresh spring air until he was sure he had been seen and everything was okay.

Bobbie Sue returned with the cake and ice cream. Everyone gathered in the executive dining room. Woody made a brief speech thanking them for their cooperation thus far. He told them that Doc Holmes would begin interviews at 12:00 the next day. He asked Roberta to type a list showing the respective order and time for each interview. He told them not to be afraid to provide factual information and cautioned them that the statements they made would be sworn and become part of OBM's official file at headquarters. He explained the role Sara West would play and said if they had any questions during the interview, they should talk to Sara. Sara would ask Doc Holmes to leave the room so that she and the interviewee could talk privately. He told them, "Sara is here to protect your rights and will direct you in the proceedings." Everyone seemed relaxed and ready to go. They enjoyed the cake and ice cream, had some fun, and for the moment forgot the problems related to Lawrance and the complex.

About 2:00, Woody asked Roberta to call Nange Rogers to the office. Nange had worked for the company for over forty-five years and was the only employee who had worked at the complex under three different managers. Roberta told Woody that he was an honest, loyal, hardworking man. He had been treated like a personal servant by Lawrance and the manager before. Woody was anxious to talk to him. When Nange entered the room he quickly removed his cap and stood near the door. Woody invited him to come in and sit down and asked if he wanted something to drink.

"No sir, thank you." Woody could see how nervous Nange was and began talking to him about the weather, gardening, fishing, and anything that popped up. The man was very uncomfortable. Woody asked if he had ever been in that office. Nange replied, "No sir, I ain't allowed in here."

"You can come in here anytime you want to. All you have to do is let Tommy know when you want to see me and let him make the arrangements for you."

"Thank you, sir and could I please have that glass of water now?"

"Wait, don't leave; take this glass and pour some from the pitcher on the conference table." Nange was hesitant, so Woody got up to pour the water and handed it to him.

"That water tastes mighty fine." Nange's shirt was wringing wet with sweat.

"How about a fan?

"Yes sir."

"Roberta, would you get a small fan and set it on the table?" A few minutes later she came in with the fan.

Nange stood up and greeted her, "How are you, Miss Roberta?"

Roberta replied, "Fine," and set the fan

on the table.

Nange grabbed the cord and said, "Let me plug it in for you, Miss Roberta." The fan came on and Roberta set it so it would oscillate back and forth moving the air in the room. Woody thanked Roberta and she went back to her office. Woody asked Nange to have a seat and make himself comfortable.

Nange appeared to be calming down somewhat, but he was still very uneasy. He didn't know what "the bossman" wanted and was terrified just being in the big office. They talked about Nange's family of twelve kids, five boys and seven girls. Woody asked why so many kids. Nange told him he had eighteen brothers and sisters, and it was natural for him to have a big family also. They talked about fishing, baseball, and working at the complex.

Woody asked Nange to start at the beginning of his career and tell him some of the things he had done at the complex while working for OBM. The old gentleman began, "I started working here in 1934 and have worked here ever since. I've done practically everything around the complex that requires a strong back. I know about everything and everybody. One of my greatest remembrances was the day the President of the United States came to visit. The roads were lined with people waving American flags and having fun."

"How many more years do you want to work, Nange?"

"I've already worked forty-seven years and I'd like to make fifty."

"That certainly seems possible. What's your secret to long life?"

"Hard work every day except Sunday. You don't have to work on Sunday. That's the Lord's day and that is the day to go to church. For the last ten years I've been a house and yard boy for the other two bossmen. I didn't like that 'cause I wanted to work with the other men. I never told the other bossmen I didn't want to work in the house or yard 'cause I was afraid to. I didn't want to lose my job, but I didn't like being separated from the other workers. I almost quit going to church 'cause they joked at me in front of my family, and you know a man needs to be proud in front of his family."

Nange began to tell how his weekly work was laid out for him. Each Monday morning he would wash dishes all morning long. The manager and his family would make a mess all week and leave it for Nange to clean up.

"How many dishes did you wash on Monday morning?"

"Mr. Woody, I have washed one hundred thirty-three plates on some Mondays."

"Wow! What do you think of that?"

"It's awful for Mr. Lawrance and Mrs. Juanita to make such a mess in front of the kids. Why, they won't know any better when they grow up." Nange just shook his head.

"Okay, what happens after Monday?" He worked hard usually through Wednesday cleaning the house and washing and ironing clothes. Thursday, Friday, and Saturday were usually spent outside in the yard and gardens. The yard was cut, raked, and fertilized each week. The flower beds were weeded each week and new mulch added as necessary.

"When was the last time you worked

with the men?"

"Several years, maybe as long as ten years." Nange said he had to wash and wax the manager's private car and truck once a week no matter if it rained or shined.

"How did you receive your pay check?"

"Every two weeks."

"Did Lawrance ever pay you in cash or with a personal check?"

"No sir. Mr. Lawrance always paid me with a company check."

"Did you ever think you were accepting illegal payments?"

"No sir, I worked for my pay."

"I'm sure you work hard for your pay, but OBM doesn't hire domestic help or personal servants. Can any other employees back up your story?"

"They all know what I've done for the last few years, but I don't know if they will talk or not, but sometimes others worked with me in the gardens. Are you going to fire me?"

"I'm not going to fire you. You will rejoin the work force later in the week."

Nange stood up and told Woody he would gladly join the work force and do his part. He left and Woody sat in his chair wondering how many situations such as this Doc Holmes would eventually uncover.

The workday was over, so Woody closed the blinds signaling his departure from the office. After supper that night he and Jay Cee watched a ball game on television. Neither was very talkative; both seemed to be in a rather pensive mood. Jay Cee recognized that Woody was becoming more exhausted each day because he was carrying such a heavy workload. He asked, "Is Lawrance Wilson still employed with OBM?"

"Yes, he is working in corporate headquarters."

"Has Lawrance been in contact with any of the employees at the complex?"

"Lawrance has called Roberta and some of the men in the work force."

"Do you know what transpired in the conversations?"

"Lawrance told Roberta that I am trying

to get rid of him. Roberta also said that Lawrance was trying to organize the work force to go on strike."

Jay Cee listened carefully. After Woody drifted off to sleep, Jay Cee called the Chairman and relayed all of the information Woody had just provided. He also updated him regarding the tail he had requested on one of the employees. "Is there any chance we can speed up the process so that a tentative decision can be made regarding Lawrance Wilson's future?"

The Chairman thought for a moment and said, "I'll finalize the paperwork on Lawrance before noon tomorrow."

"Do you think he could be placed under court order precluding him from entering the field complex?"

"I think that's reasonable, Jay Cee. He really should not be allowed to enter the administrative offices, the control bays, or any of the control centers."

"I'm concerned for Woody but I also think we should consider the possibility that an act of sabotage might be on Lawrance's mind."

"I'll take care of all the legal requirements, Jay Cee. Call me at 10:00 in the morning for an update. I think I'll have good news for both you and Woody."

Jay Cee felt better knowing Lawrance Wilson would be placed under court order. But he was also well aware that Wilson's network of influence was so extensive that just preventing him from being on the premises might not prevent sabotage against OBM.

24

The next morning Woody got up, showered, shaved, dressed, then knocked on Jay Cee's door. Jay Cee told him about the previous night's conversation with the Chairman and explained what would probably happen next. Woody was glad to hear the news and left the motel in time to arrive at the complex on schedule.

The usual morning greetings were exchanged, and Woody went to his office. Roberta tapped on his door. "Lawrance Wilson is holding for you on line one." Even saying the name brought a look of disgust to Roberta's pretty face.

Woody thought Lawrance was at headquarters but he soon discovered the former manager was at home not more than two miles from the complex.

"Woody, I want to come to the office and get my personal belongings out of my desk."

"I thought you were at headquarters. What are you doing back in Bakersfield?"

"I didn't want to stay away from my family any longer."

Woody understood that because he had not seen his own family in three weeks. He missed spending time with his two sons and had thought about asking them to join him at the motel for a weekend. Joseph, his older son, loved to fish and maybe they could find some time to wet a hook.

"Lawrance, I'll get back to you within an hour and let you know. Give me a number where I can reach you." He quickly jotted down a phone number and hung up.

Immediately Woody left the office, drove to a pay phone, and called the Chairman. Like Woody, he thought Lawrance was still working at headquarters. "It doesn't really matter, though. I've just signed the papers to fire

Lawrance. They will be hand delivered at noon today by the vice-president for personnel, Simon Rawlins."

"Lawrance wants to come in and get some things from his desk. What do you think?"

"Stall him until the VP arrives, then the two of you can accompany Lawrance to the office."

Woody called Lawrance from the pay phone and told him to be at the office at noon. Lawrance had no way of knowing the surprise that would be waiting for him.

About 11:45 Simon Rawlins arrived with the papers to fire Lawrance. To Woody's surprise and delight he was accompanied by a personnel specialist, the security manager, Tony Thayer, and the Chairman's chief legal officer, Sam Alexander. They sat in Woody's office discussing the situation until about 12:15 when Lawrance arrived at the administrative office and asked to see Woody. He was escorted down the hall by Bobbie Sue. As Lawrance entered Woody's office she turned to leave. Woody asked her to stay.

"In order for you to gain access to the locked desk drawer, Lawrance, you will be required to make a list of everything you remove. Bobbie Sue will type the list for your review and signature. Then she will make copies for the VP, legal counsel, security manager, and me.

As Lawrance unlocked the drawer, the attorney reviewed each document as it was removed. Lawrance made his list, signed it, and said, "I didn't find what I was looking for so I'll leave."

Simon Rawlins, VP for personnel, stepped forward and said, "Oh, by the way, I've got some papers for you. You need to sign acknowledging receipt. You have seven days in which to respond to the letter if you so desire. If no response is received from you within that time period the decision included will be considered final."

Lawrance looked like he had been hit in the head with a baseball bat. He turned pale, began to shake all over, and broke out in a cold sweat. He was so nervous and angry he could hardly hold a pen to sign his name. He grabbed his copy of the firing paper and left the room immediately. As he passed Woody he stopped, looked him in the eye and said between gritted teeth, "If you think this is the end of this you're wrong. And you will regret it." Then he stormed out of the building. When Lawrance got to his car he sat for several minutes reading and rereading the letter.

OBM had pulled a smooth, smart move. Lawrance thought he would come to the office and cause trouble. He left like a whipped pup with his tail between his legs.

Toasts to each other for a job well done were in order. Since they had no wine, everyone raised their Cokes in toast. Lawrance had suffered defeat at last. Simon asked Woody, "How are the interviews going?"

"I have never seen an organization with so many employees who didn't know what their actual duties were. We've completed about fifty percent of the interviews and only about five percent of the workers have a clear idea of what they were originally hired to do. Simon, when did the personnel office last conduct a review of the employees' actual work assignments?"

"Oh, wow, it's been several years I guess."

"Company policy requires a review every two years, I believe."

"You're right but higher priority work has prevented me from conducting the reviews. There are only so many hours in the day, Woody."

"I'm going to speak with the Chairman to rearrange personnel priorities and get them back in line." Simon apologized for his insensitive remarks and assured Woody that action would be taken to correct any similar problems elsewhere in OBM. Woody accepted the apology and withdrew his threat to call the Chairman.

Woody turned his attention to Tony. "What procedures should we follow if Lawrance returns to the complex?"

"The first thing is to alert the sheriff's office."

"I don't know how much help we'd get there. They're involved in this. We aren't sure how high up yet or how extensive but I don't trust them." Although Woody did not mention the situation with Roberta a couple of years ago, it was on his mind. "Do you have another suggestion?"

"The U.S. Marshals would be the next best bet."

"Why would the Marshals be interested in this situation?"

The security officer explained that several violations outside of OBM policy could come into focus, such as violation of civil rights, possession and selling of drugs and maybe even murder.

"Would you touch base with the Marshal's office and explain the situation? I don't want to call them unless they have been fully briefed on the circumstances."

"Sure, I can do that right now." The security manager went to the next office to call the Marshal's Office.

Woody turned once again to Simon. "What does the Chairman want to come out of this investigation?"

Simon answered very quickly and directly saying, "The Chairman wants this investigation to go forward with as much vigor as ever. He's looking for evidence that will stick to use in a criminal case. He wants Lawrance to pay dearly for what's gone on here."

The company had a long and glorious history of professional public service, and one SOB was not going to destroy that reputation. Simon said, "The public will know how OBM deals with criminals. This will be a test, landmark case, and full power will be exerted. The actions to be taken against Lawrance will be the severest OBM can impose and will serve as a reminder to all other field managers to keep their operations clean and above board. Managers are expected to become good neighbors and take an active role in community affairs. They are expected to serve on volunteer boards, become involved in little league associations and generally set an example of public service that will encourage others to become involved also." The example set by Lawrance, however, was one the Chairman wanted to remove from existence.

The Chairman wanted a squeaky clean, strong individual to succeed Lawrance so that

OBM's hard-earned image could be quickly restored. He wanted the next manager to work hard at cleaning up the tainted image left by Lawrance after he had done his part by prosecuting the crooked manager to the hilt. Woody knew exactly such a person currently working at another complex managed by OBM. He realized, however, that a lot of work had to be done before that person could be brought in as the new manager.

Woody told the group that he felt the employees were ready to spill their guts on Lawrance. Although some were still loyal to Lawrance, Woody believed they would cooperate and provide incriminating information. Tony returned to the room, gave Woody a piece of paper with a phone number and name on it. He told Woody this individual was a senior member of the Marshal's force and was ready to respond immediately if needed. The official had been fully briefed and understood that they would play a part in this whole mess once the investigation ended. He was prepared to intervene at any time. Woody already felt better about continuing the investigation.

"Tony, would you inspect the exterior security system to make sure it is sufficient and operational?"

Before leaving the room Tony made one suggestion. "I want you to install a back-up electrical system to all outside gates and fences. I'm a little concerned that Lawrance might try to disable the one in place. If he succeeds he would have access to the inside of the complex.

"I will issue a work order to get the electrical engineering staff working on installation of a backup system right away. Anything else?"

"All locks should be replaced."

"That was done the first day I arrived here."

Tony went outside to begin a physical inspection of the security gates and fence.

Simon was getting a little bit upset because he had intended to return home before nightfall. "Woody, I think I'm going to take the jet and return to headquarters without Tony. I have things to do I can't wait around here for him all day."

"Well, Simon, why don't you call the Chairman and let him know?"

Simon thought about that call and decided not to make it. "I guess it won't matter if I arrive home after dark. Woody knew the Chairman would not have approved of the VP leaving Tony until he had completed his surveillance.

Woody's normal quitting time had passed and he needed to let Jay Cee know everything was okay. The stretching exercise worked well a couple of days ago when Bobbie Sue used his car so he excused himself from the group and walked out on the front porch. He began to stretch while looking toward the parking lot. He did not see Jay Cee so he could only hope that his friend had seen him. After about ten minutes he returned to the executive conference room and began working on the pile of paperwork on the table. Simon had relaxed so much, he had fallen asleep in his chair. Woody attacked the stack of steadily growing papers on his desk ignoring the snoring Simon. About dusk Tony returned from his inspection of the grounds.

"Everything looks okay. If you get that back-up electrical system in place you should be in good shape."

"Thanks for checking it out, Tony. I feel a little better knowing our security is in order. It looks like we're going to have to wake your buddy up so you guys can get back to headquarters."

Woody drove them to the airport with Jay Cee following a few car lengths behind. Before they boarded the company jet, Woody shook hands with the pair and thanked them individually for their assistance. He asked that they brief the Chairman when they returned to headquarters. He watched the plane taxi to the runway then take off, climbing steeply into the cloudy Mississippi sky before it disappeared in the darkness. Soon all he could see was the flashing flying lights and it was not long before they were gone too.

Woody returned from the airport to the motel with Jay Cee again following his customary distance behind. Woody looked forward to the day the security could be reduced. As much as he enjoyed the chance to renew his friendship with Jay Cee, all the cloak and dagger routine was getting old. After supper Woody told Jay Cee that Lawrance had been fired. He congratulated Woody and told him to relax and enjoy the evening adding that it looked like this mess would be cleaned up. Woody had brought a briefcase full of paperwork to get done and wanted to be left alone.

25

Woody was ready to go to work at 5:00 a.m. As he started downstairs and approached his car he remembered what Jay Cee had told him that first night. It seemed like ages ago. So much had happened and he had learned so much. Some of it he would have preferred to have never known but he was now more determined than ever to see Lawrance pay for his crimes.

Woody turned around and went back through his room into Jay Cee's, who was just getting out of bed. "I almost left without checking with you, Jay Cee."

"Based on what had happened yesterday it's a good bet that someone had messed with your car." He dressed hurriedly and slipped out of his room, going through the outside opening to the opposite side of the motel.

For the first time Woody discovered how Jay Cee always got out unseen. The bodyguard put on a ski mask and jogging clothes and made his way to the top of the motel. From that vantage point he could survey the entire parking lot. Everything looked okay so he descended to the parking lot and very carefully looked for any leaks under Woody's vehicle. He checked each door, the trunk lid and the hood. Everything looked normal but he wanted to be on the safe side.

Jay Cee reentered his room from the opposite side of the motel. He gave Woody keys to another car parked in front of the restaurant. "Go ahead to breakfast and stay in the restaurant until I give you the signal that everything is okay. Then we'll go to the office just like any other day. I'll be a few car lengths behind you."

"Do you really think something might have been done to the car?"

Jay Cee smiled. "They pay me big bucks to make sure nothing has."

Everything went according to plan. After Woody was safely at the office, Jay Cee went to a pay phone and called the security office in the metroplex. He wanted a couple of guys to come inspect Woody's car to make sure nothing was wrong. If the vehicle was safe to drive, they would wait until Woody returned to the motel and swap cars. If anything was wrong, they would take the car to the metroplex for closer inspection. Woody had no idea anything was going on and went about his work.

Doc Holmes called and wanted to come by the office and talk to Woody at 10:00. Bobbie Sue met him in the front administrative office and directed him to the conference room where Woody was waiting. It was evident from their conversation that Doc knew all about Woody. He was surprised at the details of his life that Doc was aware. Woody, on the other hand, knew only what the Chairman had told him about Doc.

The investigator was ready to get to work and had a long series of questions to ask Woody which seemed like an investigation in itself. Questions about work relationships between Woody and the staff helped fill in missing information.

"Certain employees are more helpful than others and, in fact, some were very difficult, Doc.

"Do you have the employees grouped as I requested?"

"Yes, here is the breakdown in groups. Each group has been assembled just as you asked." Woody pulled a folder from his middle desk drawer and handed it to Doc.

Doc leafed through the several sheets, occasionally stopping to ask if certain ones had been interviewed. "How many more interviews do you intend to conduct?"

"No more, unless you think it's necessary for me to continue."

"No, that's fine. I'll take over from here."

"That's a relief. I haven't enjoyed that part at all. I'll tell the Chairman what arrangements we've agreed to."

"Great, he won't have a problem with that. I had a long discussion with him and told him what I planned to do. Could you see that I get an employee payroll and a work schedule? I'll be flexible on the work schedules and fill in replacements as necessary to fill voids created by the investigation process." The worst case would require replacement of an entire shift because Doc would interrogate individually in one room and retain the rest of a shift of employees in another room until all had been questioned.

Doc was set up in a local motel. He told Woody he wanted to start the investigations at 7:00 the next evening and work until midnight. The first interviewees would be the group identified as those "knowing the most."

He would compare questions for the later groups as he learned from the first group. Doc wanted the group most hostile and disloyal to OBM last. "I want to develop all the background information so that I can apply adequate pressure to secure complete and accurate confessions."

"Exactly what kind of pressure are you planning?"

"Don't worry. Sara will be in the room to make sure nobody gets too much abuse. The interrogation room has one chair for the interviewee and one desk and one chair each for Sara and me. It has a ceiling fan with a light above it. The fan is set on slow with the light shining on the interviewee seated directly beneath it. There will be no other lights on in the room. The slowly turning fan blades reflect the light and cause light and dark spots to occur."

"Sounds sort of ominous, just like in the movies."

Doc smiled a sly grin. "It really is intimidating when you're seated in the hot seat trying to answer questions."

"When will Sara would join you?"

"She will also arrive promptly at 7:00."

"Do I need to be available?"

"Not until tomorrow. I'll call you when I need you."

"The supplies and typing support will be available when you need them."

Doc smiled his haunting, sly grin again. "I need a five-gallon water cooler filled with ice."

"I'll have it delivered to your room by 6:00 pm."

Doc thanked him and departed. Woody leaned back in his big leather chair. He was feeling drained as though he had been put through an interrogation himself. He turned around and looked out his window just as Doc was driving away.

The meeting with Doc Holmes had taken Woody by surprise. His intimidating manner and coarse language were totally unexpected. The big man sat in front of Woody, pulled his pants legs up, and nonchalantly scratched his ankle and calf as he asked questions. He used abusive language and Woody knew he would scare the hell out of the people being interviewed. Woody was caught so off-guard by Doc's mannerisms that he had not extended an invitation to have lunch together. Neither had he mentioned what had happened the night before. Woody almost felt sorry for the employees who would be interrogated by this guy. Doc was overwhelming and scary. Woody had to catch his breath for a minute and collect his thoughts.

Woody called Roberta and told her to contact the first group of employees to be interviewed. She set up a specific schedule beginning at 7:00 the next evening. Each person was allotted thirty minutes. They would all be detained, however, until midnight. If the interrogations went faster they would be released earlier. No matter how long it took, none would be released until all had testified.

For the next two days employees were given an opportunity to make voluntary statements. Those who refused to make statements were immediately given a refresher course in personnel procedures that required them to cooperate with an official investigation. Afterwards, all employees agreed to make statements.

Before the investigation ended, more than fifty instances of violation of company policy were logged. Signed statements were secured from seventy-eight employees and local citizens. Roberta had already established the priority so all she had to do was tell the employees what time to show up. She pointed out that adjustments would have to be made to maintain a fully staffed evening shift. Woody asked her to make the necessary arrangements and within an hour she returned to Woody's office with a revised work schedule.

"Thanks, Roberta. I really appreciate all the help you've provided. You are doing another great job."

Roberta smiled a modest thank you.

"I noticed you put your name first on the interrogation list. Why do you want to be first?"

"I want to get my licks in on Lawrance early. He abused me sexually and mentally and I have some very strong comments to make. I want to set the tone."

Woody was amused by her comment and knew it was the "jilted woman's scorn" coming out. He told Roberta he hoped she could withstand the intense interrogation and should be prepared to describe the extent of her knowledge about any crimes committed by or allowed by Lawrance. Personal situations should not be the main thrust of her comments to Doc. If those situations in some way forced her to be an accomplice she should so state. However, the graphic sexual descriptions should be deleted.

Roberta chuckled at that. "One confession regarding that dark part of my life is enough. I feel much better that I have told someone and now I can concentrate on company matters." She looked much more relieved and relaxed than she had been since Woody arrived at the complex.

Woody looked further down the interrogation schedule. A pattern of comment, support, and verification was definitely evident. Roberta had tilted the scales in favor of OBM. Woody asked if she could work the upcoming weekend. He said he would like to leave Bakersfield on Friday evening and return late Sunday. He wanted to visit his family and try to alleviate the fear they were facing. Roberta said she could work.

Woody planned to have a subordinate supervisor in charge but would not do that unless she also agreed to work. Roberta said, "Tommy should be left in charge. I trust him and he will do what I ask him to do. Everything will be under control with both of us on duty."

"Contact Tommy and ask him to come to the office. I want to talk to him about working next weekend but I want to be certain that Tommy understands exactly what is expected."

It wasn't long until Roberta was ushering Tommy into Woody's office. They reviewed safety and security precautions at the complex. Tommy said, "I appreciate the confidence you've placed in me. I'm somewhat reluctant to accept the responsibility, but feel I need to in order to improve my standing with OBM." If I accept this responsibility, will any of the charges against me be dropped?"

"Your stock will increase sharply in the eyes of the Chairman if you conduct yourself in a responsive and responsible manner."

"I want to accept the responsibility but I'm afraid some of Lawrance's boys will call me a turncoat and I'll suffer the consequences. They know Lawrance and I were involved in private farming operations and realize that relationship could be grounds for removal from OBM."

Tommy was really in a dilemma. He wanted to do everything he could to improve his chances of keeping his job, but at the same time he knew he would have to face the employees not only at work but in the community as well. He needed time to weigh the costs of his action and asked Woody if he could give his answer the next morning.

"Sure that will be okay." Woody recognized the major problem Tommy faced and told him, "I have faith that you'll make the right decision. Let me know what you've decided early tomorrow."

"Thanks, this won't be easy." Tommy left the room in a very somber mood with some heavy decisions to make.

"Roberta, what group did you put Tommy in for the interrogations?"

"He knows a lot but is reluctant to volunteer information. Doc Holmes will have to pull information out of him."

"Tommy will be no match for Doc because he will know enough about Tommy's and Lawrance's joint operation to scare the pants off him. Doc will give him an opportunity to confess and if he doesn't take it, strong arm tactics will be used to get a confession. Tommy can do himself a big favor if he lays his cards on the table without coercion." Woody hoped Roberta would pass this information on to Tommy and convince him to cooperate willingly.

Tommy was the first black man to reach a supervisory level this high in OBM and was looked on as a model for other blacks to follow. The question he had to ask was, "If I cooperate with OBM in this massive investigation, will the black employees and black community look upon me as an Uncle Tom?" Tommy had a lot of soul searching to do before returning to the complex and facing Woody the next morning.

When it was time for Woody to close his office for the day, he gave Jay Cee the signal and proceeded to the parking lot. He felt good driving to the motel. He had extended a helping hand to a key employee accused of major wrongdoings and hoped Tommy would take advantage of the opportunity that had been presented to him. If he didn't Woody knew the Chairman would pursue the foreman's removal just as vigorously as he had Lawrance's. Tommy had been suckered by Lawrance and Woody didn't want him to lose his job because of the self-serving former manager.

Woody arrived at the motel, parked in his usual spot, and entered his room. Shortly afterward Jay Cee knocked on the connecting door. "Woody, have you been contacted by the other side today?

"No, things seem to be pretty quiet so I want to go home for the weekend. I'll call the Chairman tonight to discuss my plans."

"Who will be in charge while you're gone?"

Woody told him about his conversation with Tommy and said, "Since you're a black man, can you understand the dilemma Tommy is facing?"

"I don't know Tommy but unless he is a super strong human being he cannot accept the offer. It would be easier for him to do what you want him to do in Chicago, than in Bakersfield, Mississippi."

Woody looked puzzled by that statement. "He could really help himself if he could withstand the pressure from the black community."

"Since you are not a member of a minority race, it is impossible for you to understand what mental anguish Tommy is going through."

"I guess you're right, Jay Cee. I'm hungry, I want to go to the restaurant and eat everything on the menu."

After supper Woody returned to his room to call the Chairman and discuss plans for the upcoming weekend. Woody told him that Tommy and Roberta would be on duty and, if they needed to, could reach him by phone at his home in Walnut Hills. The Chairman agreed saying that Roberta and Tommy were good choices but he also wanted to add some undercover security from the metroplex.

Woody signaled Jay Cee to pick up the phone in his room so all three could talk. The Chairman had some questions for Jay Cee and asked Woody to put him on the line. He asked, "What do you think about Woody driving three hours by himself Friday and again on Sunday?"

"I have no intention of letting Woody drive by himself. I'll also talk to the State Highway Patrol and keep in radio contact with them as we travel. I'll ride with Woody to Walnut Hills and return. I can get a small van from the metroplex and remove one seat so that I can sit on the floor and not be seen."

"You think of everything."

"When you're trained by the CIA, nothing is left to chance. The four security guards who accompanied Woody and me to dinner one night will be perfect for the undercover assignment. Since they have been briefed before and have toured the complex on one of the routine guided public tours, they will blend in very well with the locals."

The Chairman chuckled. "I didn't give an order for them to tour the complex."

"That's correct, sir, but we try to take every opportunity to become familiar with every aspect of every case we work on. We work with great organizations but when it comes to security, we know what it takes to do our job much better than the organizations we protect."

"Jay Cee, I appreciate the extensive preparation you've done on this. Look, if Tommy agrees to work this weekend, Woody come on home."

After the Chairman hung up Woody turned to Jay Cee. "You don't need to ride with me, you know. Nothing is going to happen once I get out of Bakersfield. Why don't you take the weekend off?"

"I know how to do my job so don't start telling me what to do. You must realize that you are most vulnerable to attack when riding on the highway. Don't forget your run-in with the truck when you first got to Bakersfield. The highway is the best spot to make an attempt on your life. It is also the easiest place to make it look like an accident. These are the same type precautions I have taken on other occasions during my career. I am not going to let you talk me out of it. Being with you is a vacation and maybe we can take the McKenzie family to visit our old childhood play areas."

"That's a great idea and I'll look forward

to it very much." About 10:00, Woody decided to go to bed. He turned the lights out and quickly went to sleep, dreaming of spending the weekend with his family.

26

At midnight there was a loud bang on Woody's door. Immediately Jay Cee yelled to Woody to get out of the room and come to his. Woody jumped up and ran through Jay Cee's room to the connecting room on the opposite side of the motel. Several more heavy hits were made on the door then all of a sudden the plate glass window shattered. A large rock had been thrown through the window with a crudely written note that said, "Go home if you love your family. If you don't drop this investigation and leave immediately you will never see them again." Jay Cee ran to the roof of the motel where he saw an old pickup truck speeding out of the parking lot onto the highway and proceeding east. He was unable to get a license number or good description of the truck. It was an older model with faded paint similar to the one that had tried to force Woody off the road.

Jay Cee told Woody to call the motel innkeeper and the sheriff's department. The innkeeper came immediately and in less than five minutes the sheriff's deputy arrived. Woody gave him the details of the attack and the note.

"I'll alert the highway patrol and the surrounding counties. Let me keep this note for evidence."

"In the thirty years I've been in the motel business, I've never seen anything like this." The motel manager scratched his head and walked through the room picking his way over the pieces of strewn glass. "Do you want to move to the other side of the motel?"

Woody said, "I would prefer not to change rooms if the plate glass window can be fixed in one day. I want to show these people that they are not going to run me off."

"I understand, the window will be replaced before the end of the day."

"My number's in the book if you fellas have any more trouble." The deputy got in his car and drove behind the convenience mart next door. Pulling a cigarette lighter from his pocket, he set fire to the crumpled note and watched it burn.

Woody removed his belongings from the room so the repairmen could begin as soon as possible. Jay Cee contacted the security group in the metroplex who in turn contacted the local FBI office and reported the incident. Before daybreak two FBI agents were in town talking with the sheriff. They impressed on him the urgency of locating the pickup truck and occupants as soon as possible.

At 5:00 a.m. Jay Cee called the Chairman and reported the rock throwing incident. The Chairman was quite shaken by this turn of events and considered closing the complex and bringing Woody back to headquarters. He knew the situation could get nasty and escalate to more than a battle of words; more physical violence was sure to follow. The Chairman asked, "How is Woody coping with the situation?" Jay

Cee said, "Woody's doing okay, all things considered. He's alert and razor sharp and since his determination has its roots in the banks of the Sunflower River, he will resist all efforts to convince him to give up." The Chairman asked Jay Cee to put Woody on the phone.

"Why don't we call this off and bring you home?"

"I'm even more intent on seeing this situation through to the end. I won't consider leaving the complex and these loyal, courageous people. I'm canceling my plans to go see my family this weekend."

"Woody, there is no need to cancel your plans. Your family needs you as much or more than the employees at the complex."

"To leave now, even though plans were made before the attack occurred, would give the opposition a false signal. I want to keep the security folks in place just as planned and I also want to stay. Besides, I don't want to lead them to my family."

"Don't feel that you have to risk your well being for the sake of the company. And don't do anything stupid." "I'll do everything in my power to protect my people."

"I applaud your efforts and dedication, but just take extra precautions."

"I'll call my family and explain the situation."

The Chairman agreed and told Woody if he changed his mind, let him know. Woody thanked him.

Jay Cee overheard the conversation and patted him on the back. He said, "You're one hard nut. Most people faced with your situation would turn tail and run."

"Don't forget, you had to make me get out of bed earlier this week."

"Yeah, but this is different. I thought we were dealing with angry people, not vindictive people. Anyone who would do all of this has malicious intent." Jay Cee's comments, if intended to make Woody feel better, were having the opposite impact. Woody's impression of a vindictive person was an individual who would do anything to get even. Jay Cee suggested that Woody consider spending less time in his office which had the large plate glass window exposed on the outside wall.

"I can move my operation to an interior office in the complex."

"I want to pose as a salesman and come by the office for a visit. I'll inspect the interior office to be sure that it's not bugged or in some other way unsuitable for you to occupy."

"How can we pull this off without anyone catching on?"

"Just leave that to me."

He was sure the loyal employees would also suffer harassment. They previously expressed fear of reprisal tactics Lawrance might use. Woody realized he was learning too much. He and others in OBM were getting too close and too deeply involved in other people's activities. Armed with that knowledge, OBM could be expected to take decisive actions that would result in criminal charges being brought against Lawrance.

Jay Cee suggested that he go to breakfast early and on to the complex. Woody needed to break his normal routine just in case the opposition had plans for another attack along the highway.

"I'll grab a couple of doughnuts and coffee and be ready to leave in fifteen minutes."

"Fine, I'll go inspect the vehicles and be ready to follow you."

Jay Cee dressed in a business suit so he could inspect Woody's office beginning promptly at 8:00. He gave Woody a business card to leave with the receptionist so she would be expecting a salesman.

"You amaze me Jay Cee." Woody put the card in his pocket.

After picking up breakfast, Woody returned to the room to wait for Jay Cee. Fifteen minutes passed and Jay Cee had not returned. Woody was getting anxious. What had happened to his friend? He moved to the window and, without touching it, attempted to look out but could only see the rear portion of his car. He waited a few more minutes becoming more tense as each second ticked by. Finally Jay Cee returned to the room, out of breath and visibly shaken. Woody looked at him quizzically and asked, "What's going on?"

Jay Cee was trying to catch his breath and regain his composure. He told Woody he had gone about his usual routine, going first to the roof to take a look at the entire parking lot. Everything looked okay as it had for the last two weeks, so he went down his portable ladder, removed and stored it. Carefully he went to the opposite end of the parking lot, his eyes searching every parked car. He approached Woody's car and everything looked normal. He checked the tires, the hood, the trunk lid, and under the car.

As he looked at the passenger door, he found smudges that he knew had not been there the night before. Although concerned, he was not yet alarmed. Since robberies had occurred at the motel before, he figured that the smudges were probably related to a thwarted robbery attempt. However, trained as he was, Jay Cee did not stop his inspection. He had a set checklist of things to do similar in nature to the safety check process a pilot goes through before takeoff. After the outside inspection, Jay Cee always inserted the key and unlocked the driver's door.

Everything appeared to be okay, so he opened the door and looked in. So far, other than the smudges on the door, everything looked normal. Jay Cee sat in the driver's seat, inserted the key in the ignition, and turned it.

The engine started without hesitation. He let it warm up for a few seconds, then turned the motor off and stepped out of the car. As he slammed the front door, something in the rear floorboard moved and caught his eye. He quickly looked again and saw an enormous rattlesnake crawling out from under the driver's seat. Although on the outside of the vehicle and safely away from the snake, Jay Cee was shaken by the close call. He had a healthy respect for and tremendous fear of all snakes. The adrenalin was pumping through his veins as he ran upstairs to tell Woody what had just happened. They decided to call the sheriff's office to remove the snake. Woody left his car keys with the manager and decided to use one of the other company cars.

Woody was leaving the motel just as the deputy arrived. He stopped and told the deputy what a close call he had. The deputy grinned and told Woody, "You sure have your share of trouble."

"Nothing I can't handle. You better be careful."

"In my line of work you have to be careful. Do you have any idea how that snake got in your car?"

"Maybe there's a hole open to the outside under the car, but I didn't look around very much after seeing the snake."

Woody saw Jay Cee in the rearview mirror. He wanted Woody to start moving. A stopped target is easier to hit than a moving one and the element of surprise, being ahead of his normal schedule, was being lost. Woody turned into traffic and headed for the office. This morning he was thirty-five minutes early. As he drove he vividly remembered how terrified he was the night the pickup truck bumped him. Although the driving conditions were better, he approached every curve well under the posted speed limit. The sun was rising but the shade from the huge trees on both sides created lots of dark spots on the road. Woody kept his headlights on high beam and was especially observant as cars approached from the front and rear. He continuously searched both sides of the highway for any movement. He knew Jay Cee was watching from the rear, so he felt much better this morning than he did on that rainy night when the pickup tried to knock him off the road. Not knowing what he would find around the next curve kept his attention firmly on business at hand.

27

Martha didn't sleep soundly when Woody was away. She would toss and turn most of the night, getting up several times. This night was an exception because she and Allison had exhausted themselves that afternoon shopping. Martha was awakened from her deep sleep by the ringing of the alarm clock. Since Allison was sleeping in Woody's place, Martha quickly shut off the alarm. She slowly got out of bed, slipped off her nightgown and stepped into the steaming shower. The warm water soaked her long auburn hair and cascaded down her smooth skin. Just as she finished, Martha heard the water running in the upstairs shower and she knew the boys were awake. Allison was also getting out of bed and she stumbled groggily to the bathroom. Martha said, "You take your shower and I'll start breakfast."

Martha walked into the kitchen just in time to here her mother-in-law beating on the back door frantically, screaming hysterically. About the same time Joseph heard his grandmother and came racing down the stairs yelling "What's going on?"

Trying to talk between gasps for breath, Grandmother McKenzie sobbed, "Somebody killed Baby! She's hanging on the fence. Look! I can't believe it."

As Martha tore through the door across the lawn she stopped, stunned, as she saw the limp form of their beloved pet draped, bloody and lifeless, across the back fence. Inside the house the phone rang making everyone jump. Joseph picked up the receiver but before he could say anything a strange voice said, "Have you found your dog? Just remember, if your daddy stays at Bakersfield the same thing will happen to him. We'll cut his throat and throw him in the river for turtle bait." Then all Joseph heard was a click and the eerie monotone buzz of the dial tone.

Joseph was terrified and screamed for his mother. Allison and Barry ran to him at the phone as Martha came back into the house. With tears streaming down his face, Joseph told his mother what the caller had said. She listened, then told the kids to hurry and get dressed as quickly as possible.

Joseph said, "I want to talk to Dad right now."

"Go ahead and call him. I need to talk to him too," Martha answered. Joseph grabbed the phone and started dialing the number of Woody's motel in Bakersfield.

Grandmother McKenzie sobbed, "We've got to do something with Baby; we can't leave her there. I'll take her off the fence. Where do you want me to put her?"

Martha replied, "Wait until I talk to Woody and tell him what has happened. He'll know what we should do."

The phone rang just as Woody was opening the door to leave his motel room. He lifted the receiver and heard the shaky, frightened voice say, "Daddy, please come home!"

"What's wrong, son?"

"Somebody killed Baby. It's terrible and we're scared. They said they were going to cut your throat."

"Try to calm down, son. Nobody's going to cut my throat. Let me talk to your mother." Woody tried to remain calm his anger grew at the thought of someone getting to his family this way. When Martha came to the phone his voice remained steady and confident. "Martha, what's going on?"

"He's right, Woody. Somebody killed Baby and hung her on the fence by the driveway. Right after we found him somebody called and told Joseph they would kill you if you stayed in Bakersfield. I'm scared, Woody."

"What do you mean somebody? When did all of this happen?"

"I'm not sure. Your mother was on her way over this morning and found Baby hanging there."

"Okay, I'll call the Chairman and come

home immediately. You stay home from work today and don't send the kids to school. Lock all the doors and go upstairs to the boys' bedroom. I'll be home in less than two hours. I'll ask the Chairman to have the sheriff send a deputy to stay with you until I get there. Get mother in the house with you. Leave the dog on the fence and don't let anyone in the house except the deputies. If anyone else calls with a threat, just hang up. Don't talk to them."

"Please hurry. We need you home now."

"I'm on my way. Just hold everything together until I get there."

Woody dialed the Chairman's number and called to Jay Cee in the adjoining room, "Jay Cee, come in here."

"What's going on? What's all the commotion about?"

"Listen, they're after my family. I'm calling the Chairman. Get my car ready; we're going to Walnut Hills as fast as we can."

"Do we need an escort?"

"Yes, call the highway patrol. I'll be ready to go in five minutes."

Woody explained the situation to the Chairman, called the office to let Roberta know he would be gone for the day and was ready to leave in less than the five minutes he had projected.

As Jay Cee and Woody pulled onto the Interstate headed north to Walnut Hills, they were immediately joined by a patrolman with lights flashing and siren wailing. They had driven about thirty miles when the patrolman pulled off the highway and stopped at a phone booth. As Jay Cee pulled in behind him, the officer walked up to Woody and said, "You're supposed to call the Chairman."

Woody placed the call from the phone booth. Somehow hearing the Chairman's voice had a soothing effect on him. "Woody, go to the Delta ticket counter at Non-connah airport. Two tickets will be waiting for you and Jay Cee to fly to Aspen for a few days. Your family will join you there."

"Who's going to take my place at Bakersfield?"

"Don't worry about it. I'll have a temporary replacement for you before the end of the day. Just turn around now and go to the airport. When you get to Aspen, use your company charge-card to outfit your family and Jay Cee. I'll take care of Baby and anything else that needs to be done around your house."

"Thanks. I'll call you when we arrive in Aspen."

Woody hung up the phone and took a deep breath.

28

It was not the best time of year to be in Aspen. It was also not the best of circumstances. But the plane trip had been smooth, the landing uneventful and Woody had arrived without incident. There had been lots of hugs, kisses, and even a few tears when Woody and Jay Cee met the plane carrying Martha and the kids.

The resort hotel the Chairman had booked for them lacked nothing in comfort or charm and Woody wished that he and his family had been here on a skiing vacation rather than running to protect their lives. As Woody sat on the balcony outside his room sipping a cup of coffee he kept remembering Lawrance's threat that he would get even.

The sliding glass doors parted and Martha stepped through. Woody had forgotten how beautiful she was. Even in the jogging suit that concealed the perfection of her figure her feminine form was obvious. Barefoot and with her long hair simply pulled back and tied she was still the beautiful girl Woody had fallen for so many years ago.

She gracefully slipped into the chair beside Woody's, sitting on her feet, Indian style. "I'm scared, Woody. Please ask for a transfer and let's move away from that horrible place."

"Martha, I know this has all been very rough on you. But I can't leave this job unfinished. I gave my word. You know what that means to me. I can't let the company down."

Martha could hold her anger no longer. She was fighting back tears, struggling to keep her voice from breaking. "The company? What about your family? Do you remember your family, Woody? I'm tired of hearing about your damned precious company! Does one of us have to be killed before you can let go of that company loyalty?" She was standing now with her hands clinched in fists at her side.

"Don't lecture me about family. Why do you think I've pushed so hard all these years? Why do you think I've given 110% when I felt more like giving up? Why do you think I've fought the system so hard just for a chance to advance? Don't you realize who I've done all that for? Don't you see that it's you and the kids that I've tried so hard to be a success for?"

"Woody, we don't care about success. We want you, alive and with us. Will you ever understand that you'd be a success in our eyes no matter what you did for a living?"

"It's more than just us, Martha. There are lots of families at Bakersfield who have lived their lives in fear and abuse because of Lawrance Wilson. I have to see this through. I promised I would no matter what."

"You don't have anything to prove. You can't change what the company did to your family. That's all in the past."

Woody stood too. His anger was building. "It may be in the past for you but I live it every day. I live it when I remember my father's bitterness and how his family turned its back on him. I live it every time I think of how much we had to do without just because the company shut us out. I live it every time I remember how hard it was for me to get an education when it could have been so simple. I gave my word, Martha. I knew I'd have to make sacrifices. Too many people have too much to lose if I don't see this through."

Martha lowered her voice and looked calmly at Woody. "Are you prepared to sacrifice your family? I'd rather lose you to another woman than to OBM. At least I could compete with another woman. I can't match the charms of a multi-billion dollar corporation. You had better consider what you are doing."

"Don't threaten me, Martha. Don't ask me to compromise my principles."

"It's not a threat. I just don't think I can live like this. I'm going to take a walk and check on the kids."

A few seconds later Woody heard the room door close. He stood, his hands braced on the railing gazing out across the slopes. How could he make her understand? How could he make her realize that he loved her more than anything in this world but there were some things you just couldn't walk away from?

Woody walked into the room, closing the sliding doors behind him. He felt like there was no way he could win. To stay with the job meant he might run the risk of losing Martha. To give up meant he would surely lose himself. He walked into the bathroom, undressed and turned on the shower. The soothing sound of the water spraying down filled the room. He stepped into the shower and let the force of the water hit him full in the face. He wanted to wash away the pain he was feeling, the guilt of what he was pulling his family into, the fear of what was ahead in Bakersfield and fear of losing Martha. But it was only water. Woody hadn't moved for several minutes when he heard the room door close again. He knew Martha was back and they would have to settle this.

The sound of the shower door sliding startled Woody and he turned suddenly as

Martha stepped out of her panties and into the shower. Her hair was loosened around her shoulders and a slow smile turned the corners of her full lips. Woody gasped in expectation as she came to him. He was never prepared for the effect she had on him. Standing before him, water running down her smooth firm body, she was the most beautiful sight Woody had ever seen.

"Wow. Look what I found," he said as he pulled her against him. He gently kissed each of her eyelids, then the base of her slender, graceful neck. She gazed up at Woody with that special look only he had ever had the experience of witnessing. Their lips met, gently at first. But the flow of passion was so intense that the embrace tightened and the pressure of their kiss filled each of them with uncontrollable desire. Nothing had to be said. Now, each understood the other one and Woody knew everything would be okay.

For the next hour there was no OBM, no Lawrance Wilson, no Bakersfield, no Chairman, no Mississippi, and no world. There was only love and absolute acceptance.

29

The trip to Aspen seemed only a dream now that Woody was back at Bakersfield. He wondered to himself how he became so deeply and quickly involved in such an ugly mess. Three months earlier he had returned from a twelve-month training assignment in Washington, D.C. Not once during that period of time did he encounter any physical danger. Now for him to return to his native southland and find himself embroiled in a life and death entanglement, almost on a daily basis, was incredible and unbelievable. He knew that this situation must be taken seriously and approached with great caution. Although it was not his nature to be suspicious and cautious, he was learning to question every move before he made it. He had been taught by his parents to trust people and had never had reason or cause to initially question their actions. Woody was taught to believe that people are good and can be trusted and had never encountered a situation where there was a wolf behind every tree waiting to jump out. That was just not the way it had been during the early formative years of his life.

He found it difficult to scrutinize every move he made, analyze the situation, and try to predict what others would do in certain circumstances. He had never been paranoid; he believed people were honest and always viewed others as he viewed himself. He wanted to help others, especially those less fortunate than he, and on many occasions had championed the underdog. His actions were based on sound logic and the belief that results achieved could be shared by everyone. If anyone questioned his motives, he was always willing to discuss the actions he had taken. He was a people-oriented person and enjoyed seeing others achieve their goals.

Woody continued to drive carefully toward the complex. As he approached the crossroads he saw a set of headlights approaching on the right. Since Woody had the right-of-way, he sped up slightly to be certain he passed the intersection before the other vehicle came to a stop. He looked in his rearview mirror and saw what he hoped were Jay Cee's headlights. The intersection was located in a sharp curve; therefore, Woody could not see if any traffic was approaching from the left. He sped up to about ten miles per hour over the posted speed limit. He hoped Jay Cee wouldn't become alarmed at the faster speed and think that Woody was in trouble. They had never discussed the procedure for notifying each other in case one spotted trouble, so he just hoped Jay Cee would speed up, stay his normal distance behind, and not become too alarmed. As Woody approached the intersection and passed through it, he did not see any traffic to the left. The vehicle approaching from the right turned right and managed to get between Woody and Jay Cee. Woody constantly moved his eyes from the windshield to the rearview mirror. The following vehicle maintained a constant driving distance behind Woody for about five minutes. Woody could see a second pair of headlights behind the vehicle and hoped and prayed that they belonged to Jay Cee.

All three vehicles were traveling at a higher than normal speed; however, none was speeding up or trying to close the gap. Woody was about three miles from the entrance to the complex when he met another vehicle. As they passed, the driver honked his horn as if to say hello. Woody didn't recognize the car and it was still too dark to get a good look at the occupants. Usually there was considerable traffic on the highway and maybe somebody thought they recognized the car Woody was driving. At any rate Woody was getting closer to the entrance to the complex and feeling a little bit better with each passing mile. The rising sun was beginning to light the highway more and more. This was going to be a beautiful day. As Woody turned on his left signal to turn onto the short access road to the security gate, the vehicle that had been between he and Jay Cee turned right into the large parking lot across from the complex. Woody saw Jay Cee drive by as he had in previous days, go about a mile down the road, and turn around.

Jay Cee knew that if the occupants of the middle vehicle intended to attempt anything his best position would be between them and Woody. He turned around and drove by the entrance to the complex. He could see that Woody had entered safely and was in the office. Jay Cee needed to blend in with other cars in the parking lot. That was going to be a little harder than usual since they were about thirty-five minutes earlier than normal and the parking lot was only about two-thirds full. He drove into the parking lot to about midway, putting himself in good position to observe the other vehicle that entered before him. It was now light enough to see it was an older model, rust-colored pickup, much like the one he had seen leaving the motel.

The bodyguard parked, got out, opened

his trunk, and removed a black briefcase. All the while he was observing the occupants of the pickup: three men, two black, one white, mid-thirties to early fifties. They sat in the cab of the truck facing away from the complex. Jay Cee was between two cars about seventy-five yards away with five cars between him and the truck. The briefcase he removed from the trunk was not one that a normal businessman carries. Rather it was a weapons case. He reentered his car from the passenger's side, opened the case and removed its contents. A couple of twists and clicks armed him with an assault rifle. He laid it on the seat and pretended to be reading some paperwork he had taken out of the same briefcase. He was watching every move the three men were making. They appeared to be having a rather heated argument. The driver apparently wanted to do one thing but the other two had different ideas. Evidently the early arrival of Woody had thwarted their plans and left them without a back-up. They were totally frustrated. The element of surprise had worked. The three men continued to argue. One of the passengers got out and walked to the driver's side as the driver adjusted his rearview mirror. The three exchanged words as the driver pounded his hands on the steering wheel, apparently very distraught and upset. He opened the door, stepped out, and stood with his hands on his hips, staring across the parking lot at Woody's office.

Jay Cee saw the "good ole boys" had a deer rifle in the gunrack over the seat. He was clutching the assault weapon as he opened the passenger door and stepped out. He watched the three men; the driver appeared to be getting more nervous and animated with each passing moment. He walked around the vehicle, kicking the tires, and throwing his hands up in the air. Jay Cee hoped Woody would not open the window blinds in the office. One of the men reached behind the truck seat, pulled out a pair of binoculars, and looked toward the office window. He had taken his tie and coat off to ready himself for any action that might be forthcoming.

The driver of the truck walked back to

the cab to move the deer rifle from the rack. Jay Cee lifted the assault rifle to his shoulder, sighting in on the driver. At that moment one of the security cars from the complex, on routine patrol, pulled in the parking lot. The occupants scrambled back into the truck and raced out of the lot. Jay Cee tossed the assault rifle into the seat beside him and followed the pickup truck. He moved to within ten feet of them watching closely, anticipating a sudden move. If they fired toward the office he was prepared to return the fire with his assault weapon. He was going to make sure he disabled the vehicle. He had already recorded the license plate number, color, type, and model of pickup. The truck turned onto the highway.

Jay Cee followed for a short distance then, realizing he had to stay with Woody, returned to the parking lot. He was relieved that the confrontation did not take place. Although he was prepared, he did not want to get into a gun fight. He replaced his assault rifle in its carrying case, and put his coat and tie on.

The bodyguard planned to enter the

complex under the guise of a salesman and sweep Woody's office for bugging devices. The administrative staff had not arrived, so he parked in one of the visitors parking spaces in front of the office. He waited until the receptionist opened the curtains on the front office and unlocked the door.

Now it was time for Jay Cee to make his "salesman's" entrance. He presented his business card at the front desk and the receptionist escorted him to Woody's office. Woody was seated at the conference table away from the outside window. Jay Cee looked at him and said, "I was afraid you would open those curtains and stand in front of the window."

"Hey, give me some credit too. I was watching all of that action in the parking lot from the receptionist's area. I was not about to go to my office and present those good ole boys with a target."

"I should have known you would recognize a dangerous situation and react accordingly. I need to use the phone to run a check on the pickup."

"You know this phone may be bugged, don't you?"

"No problem, if they're listening, they'll know we're hot on their trail and their actions are not going unnoticed."

"Okay, Inspector Clouseau, do your thing."

Jay Cee contacted the metroplex security office and passed the description of the pickup on to them. They would use their network system to determine the owner and might even give him a personal visit.

Jay Cee thanked them and told Woody, "Let's go look at your new office."

By this time all of the office staff had reported to work. Woody introduced Jay Cee as an office efficiency expert and furniture salesman. Woody told them Jay Cee would be looking at various rooms and furnishings in the office. He also said new furniture would be ordered and some changes in office locations would take place.

With that introduction Jay Cee would be able to move freely around the offices taking pictures and measurements. Although not in the best place to observe activities going on outside, if anything happened he would be in a better position to assist with defensive actions inside. He and Woody looked around for about an hour and Jay Cee suggested that Woody move his office to the interview room. Woody called Tommy and told him to bring a crew to the executive office to move the furniture. Within an hour Woody was settled in his new office.

30

Woody hated deceiving the office staff and felt a little bad that Jay Cee had come in under false pretenses. He wanted to tell Roberta and Bobbie Sue what was going on; however, he didn't want to tell them anything that, by their knowing, might cause a problem for them. If he asked Jay Cee about telling them, he knew what the answer would be. As a trained security person, Jay Cee wanted to keep everything secret. His philosophy was tell only the minimum number of people and tell them only the barest details.

Because Woody felt the administrative staff had cooperated one hundred percent with Woody, he thought they deserved to know what was going on. Jay Cee instructed him to answer only questions that were already public knowledge such as the All Points Bulletin on the pickup truck. Some of the employees had probably heard the early morning traffic on their scanners and knew that Woody's window at the motel had been shattered and a snake found in his car.

Jay Cee wanted to keep the connection between the pickup in the parking lot and the shattered glass window separate. Woody agreed he would answer questions but would not give any specific details. Knowing the conspiracy connection between Lawrance and the sheriff's office, he felt it would be only a matter of time before everybody knew what was going on.

Woody wondered what Doc Holmes knew and felt he should brief him on the situation. The information might be valuable to Doc during his interrogation of employees. He might bluff his way through parts of an interrogation and drop some statements here and there to see what reaction he could get. Woody called Doc's motel and the operator rang his room, but got no answer. Doc was scheduled to begin another round of interviews at 12:00. If Woody didn't hear from Doc before that time he would call the interrogation room at 12:00 sharp. Woody wanted to brief Doc so that maybe he could assist in determining the driver and owner of the mysterious pickup. Shortly before 11:00, Doc called Woody to review the list of interviewees for the 12:00 to 6:00 shift. After they confirmed the list, Woody told Doc what had happened last night and this morning.

"Do you have any strong leads or suspicions?" Doc asked.

"We have a lot of people looking, but nobody finding."

"The people who gathered outside your room that night, have you seen any of them since, or figured out who any of them might be?"

"I think one of them might be a man named Leggs Redmond and he is on the list to be interviewed today."

"I want to include Leggs in the 12:00-6:00 session so I can squeeze him. I might not get anything out of him, but I want to use him as a pony to carry information to the opposition." Doc wanted to make the bad guys think he knew a lot more than he actually did.

Woody called Roberta and told her to put Leggs on the end of today's interview list. She reminded Woody that Leggs was a strong supporter of Lawrance. Woody said, "I realize that, but Doc wants to change the order just a bit." She wanted to know if someone needed to be dropped from the list. Woody replied, "No, if the interrogations run past 6:00 p.m., that's okay."

Roberta wanted to know what was going on. She apparently had not heard anything about the search for the pickup, but she sensed something was wrong. Woody related the story to her and asked if she knew of any employees who had an old brown, rusty looking pickup.

"Leggs has one that's been 'souped' up with a big powerful engine." Woody immediately called Doc and reported this bit of news and asked Doc to be on the lookout for the pickup that evening.

Woody left the office and headed for the public phone he had used several times. As always Jay Cee pulled past him and stopped at the hill. Woody called the Chairman and had Jay Cee patched in before reporting the new information regarding the possible owner of the pickup. Jay Cee said, "I just got a make on the pickup. It belongs to a man named Redmond who lives right outside of town."

The Chairman said, "I'll have Tony Thayer contact the U.S. Marshal's office and, I must say, I'm very pleased with this turn of events." Woody thanked them and returned to his office. Roberta had once again proved how important she was.

31

Woody called Roberta to his office and told her he had changed his plans for the weekend. He was going to work and also needed her and Tommy to work. She said, "Tommy is on his way to the office and wants to talk to you about this weekend's work schedule."

When Tommy arrived the three of them sat in Woody's new office and discussed the change in plans.

Tommy was relieved and said, "I just could not have worked the weekend if you had been gone. The community pressure would have been more than I could bear."

"I want you to work the weekend anyhow."

"No problem as long as you're also on duty."

Roberta said, "I need the overtime pay so I'll be glad to work all weekend long." Everything was settled. The usual work schedules would continue as planned and the three of them would report at 7:00 both days. Tommy thanked Woody and told him he hoped he understood.

"I understand."

Roberta and Tommy left the office. Woody felt good about the discussion. He felt like he had helped two employees who had been abused by Lawrance. Although nothing could remove the pain and agony they went through under Lawrance's reign of abuse, at least they were beginning to understand that one member of OBM's top level management sympathized with their problems.

After they left Woody's office, he turned his eyes to the increasing stack of paperwork. Bobbie Sue had done a good job of arranging the work and in an effort to speed up the process, he called her to the office and asked for her assistance. He wanted her to be sure each document was signed properly and that no time was lost looking for signature blocks. He asked her to take the stack and tag each location where his signature was needed and give them back. Woody took her word that everything was in order and there would be no surprises later as he signed each document.

They worked like that until lunch time.

Bobbie Sue asked, "Do you want to share my lunch?"

"I picked up a sandwich this morning and if you don't mind, I'd like to make this a working lunch."

"Fine." About ten minutes later she returned with a lunch bag and two cold drinks. They sat at the conference table eating and working through the paperwork. By the end of the lunch period they had completed the work that had to be mailed. Although a considerable pile of paperwork remained, Woody could take more time to review what he was signing.

Bobbie Sue collected all of the documents that needed to go in the mail. She rushed them to the mail room and made sure they were stamped and sealed for delivery to the post office.

Woody continued to work on the stack of papers. It seemed like everything had been put on hold for the last several days and now he had some catching up to do. About 4:00 Jay Cee called and wanted to come by to "make some more measurements."

Woody said, "Fine," and told the receptionist that the salesman that came by earlier was on his way and she should bring him to his office when he arrived. When he arrived about fifteen minutes later, he told Woody they had some good news. The FBI had found Redmond's house out in the county, but no truck. If the pickup returned, it would be impounded and locked up at the sheriff's office.

Woody said, "Great, Doc is going to interrogate Leggs at 6:00 pm today. If Leggs cracks we'll have the type of criminal evidence the Chairman wants."

Since Jay Cee had made himself known

to the administrative work force, he saw no reason why he and Woody couldn't go to a neighboring town and have supper together. Woody agreed and said, "I want to talk to Doc immediately after his interview with Leggs because I'm excited about the possibility of a big break in the case. I need to work another hour and there is no need to go to the motel, so we can leave the complex and go directly to supper."

"I'll work in the other office for an hour and we can leave at the same time." That seemed like a good plan. The hour passed quickly. They drove to Red Bluff, a small rural town with a population of about ten thousand. As in most old towns in the south, the courthouse was located in the middle of town and over the years various shops and businesses had been established around the town square. This town was no different and had a touch of class and true southern charm to it. The restaurant Jay Cee selected was on the south side of the square in a building originally constructed as a cotton buyers and sellers market.

It had been converted to a restaurant in

the early fifties. The old red brick walls were covered with photographs of cotton farming operations as far back as the beginning of the century. Jay Cee was sure Woody would enjoy looking at the old pictures and reminiscing. It would remind him of those bygone days when they picked cotton in the fields near the Sunflower River.

Woody and Jay Cee had a wonderful time enjoying good food, drink and each other's company. They talked briefly about the huge shift in emotions they had experienced in the last eighteen hours. What a relief to be relaxed and enjoying themselves now. Their time together passed quickly. Woody left the table telling Jay Cee he wanted to call Doc.

Sara answered and Woody asked how it went and she replied, "It is still going. Doc is questioning Leggs Redmond right now."

"Have Doc stall him until we get there. We're on our way."

"Okay, but come to my room. I'll open the connecting doors and let you listen to Leggs' statement."

"Great, We'll be there in fifteen minutes." Woody went back to the table and told Jay Cee what was going on.

Jay Cee grabbed the check saying, "Let's pay this and get out of here." They were as happy as teenage boys returning from a successful hunting trip. Jay Cee and Woody arrived at Sara's motel room as excited as they could be. She let them in and told them to be quiet as she reentered the interrogation room leaving her door slightly opened. They could hear the two men talking in the next room.

Doc said, "I have a series of short questions for you, and I want you to give me complete answers to each one. Do you understand?"

"Yes sir, I understand."

Doc, realizing that Woody and Jay Cee were in the adjoining room, asked Leggs to tell him once again what type pickup truck he owned.

"I have a 1953 Chevrolet, brown with a high performance engine and running gear."

"Do you know of anyone else who has a similar vehicle?"

"No sir. I'm the only one in this part of the country with a truck that has that much power."

"Do you drive it to work every day?"

"No sir, I only use it for special occasions."

"When was the last special occasion?"

"A few days ago."

"What was special a few days ago?"

"Me and some of my friends just wanted to joy ride around town."

"Why don't you drive it to work?"

"It burns too much gas."

"Where is the truck now?"

"I guess it's at home."

Doc turned through a stack of papers and asked, "Is your home address 258 Taylor Road?"

"Yes sir."

"Where is Taylor Road?"

"About ten miles west of here off Highway 14."

"Do you lend or let anyone else drive your truck?"

"No sir. I have the only key and I keep it with me at all times."

"Do you have the key with you now?"

"Yes sir. Here it is."

Jay Cee whispered to Woody, "I've heard enough. I want to go find the truck."

Woody said, "I know where Taylor Road is. I'll leave a note for Sara telling her we're going to look for the truck and will call her later tonight."

Taylor Road crossed Highway 14 and was not hard to find. Although neither Woody nor Jay Cee knew which side 258 was located on, they turned left and tried to read the mail box numbers.

It was as dark as a house full of black cats. They drove slowly along the street looking for 258. Jay Cee remembered he had a Q-beam spotlight in the trunk. He stopped, got it out, and plugged it into the cigarette lighter socket. The light was extremely bright, almost too bright. They had driven about one-half mile and determined that they were on the wrong end of the road. They turned around, crossed Highway

14 and once again began searching for 258 on a mail box. They drove less than one-quarter of a mile when Jay Cee spotted it.

The house was located about one hundred yards away at the end of a gravel driveway. Just as Jay Cee turned into the driveway, the silhouette of a patrol car came into view, lights flashing.

The deputy climbed out of the car and said, "What in the hell are you boys doing out here?"

"I'm looking for one of my employees and his truck."

"We have his house under surveillance and don't need any interference from a city slicker like you. Anyway we've had reports about prowlers with a spotlight out here, do you know anything about that? Since you boys have been in town we've had nothing but trouble. I suggest you turn around and go back to town before you get snake bit."

Jay Cee was sitting still and quietly listening to their conversation. He was getting a little agitated at this local hot shot, smart-mouthed deputy. Woody sensed Jay Cee's feelings and told him to be calm as they drove away from the deputy. Jay Cee pulled out onto the highway and headed toward his motel. He said, "If that deputy blows this case, I'll nail his hide to the wall."

They arrived at the motel in about thirty minutes. It was late but Woody wanted to talk to Doc and Sara. When he called, they had just released Leggs. Woody told them what had happened. Doc said, "Don't worry, I'll pass the information on to the U.S. Marshals." Woody thanked Doc for his help and turned in for the night. It had been a long day.

32

Woody was awakened the next morning at 5:30 by the friendly motel operator. She was as cheerful as ever and told him to have a good day. Woody thanked her and hung up. He really did not want to get up; neither did he want another lecture from Jay Cee. He struggled up and stumbled to the shower. The hot water falling on his body felt so good he stood there for about fifteen minutes. He stepped out, dried off, and put his clothes on and went to the restaurant.

This day was starting out much better than the one before. When he returned to his room at 6:30, Jay Cee told him the vehicles had been checked and everything was okay. Woody slipped his coat on and headed for the parking lot.

The trip to the complex was uneventful. Woody arrived promptly at 7:00. Woody went to his new office and looked at the stack of papers left from the day before. Bobbie Sue stopped by and asked if he wanted a cup of coffee. Woody replied, "Yes, thank you." He sat in the big easy chair reading a memo as Bobbie Sue entered and set the coffee cup on Woody's desk. He thanked her and continued to work for about an hour until the phone rang breaking the silence. It was the Chairman.

"Doc has briefed me on the outcome of the second round of interviews."

"Doc's investigation is causing quite a stir at the complex and also in the community."

"Are any of the employees talking about Doc's interview tactics?"

"The only thing I've heard is that Doc is scaring the hell out of them. Some of his mannerisms are crude; however, they certainly are successful."

"Doc had quite a reputation when he

worked in the Atlanta police department. The toughest criminals were referred to him for interrogation. Keep a tight handle on Doc and let me know if he gets out of line. We want all of the facts, but we don't want a police brutality charge against us. Our case is solid against Lawrance and we don't want anyone to do anything that would jeopardize it."

"I'll be available to hear any complaints if someone wants to make one. Thanks, again, for your support." He hung up the phone.

Woody looked at the list of the third group Doc was to start interviewing at 12:00. The first name, Jeff Wilkerson, was a former assistant to Lawrance. Woody wondered why Roberta had put him on that list and not one of the earlier ones. He called Roberta and asked, "Why did you put Jeff on the third list?"

"He was as guilty as Lawrance, although not as arrogant. He was also a victim of Lawrance's actions, but he was in a position to do something about it, yet chose not to." Roberta was upset with Jeff, but at the same time, felt sorry for him. "He's a weak man and should never have been put in a position of authority."

"What does Jeff have to hide.

"Doc has all the information and will nail him with it." Roberta sounded resentful and angry. True enough Jeff was a non-descript type person, but a thief - that was hard for Woody to believe.

"Okay, thanks."

Doc called to review the interview listing just as he had done the day before. "Everything is in order and I'm ready for round three."

"Do you need any assistance in the way of typing, copying, or supplies?"

"I need to get some more statement forms. If someone can deliver them to the interrogation room before 12 o'clock, I would appreciate it."

"I'll send Bobbie Sue to the printing shop in Red Bluff and have the copies made within a couple of hours."

"That would be great, I have enough for this round, but I'll need some for the next one."

"Has Leggs made any confessions about the rock throwing incident, the rattlesnake incident, or the bumping incident.

"No, but it's just a matter of time. I want to interview Leggs again with the fourth group, but don't alert him just yet. I want to give him enough time to talk to Lawrance and his supporters."

"Do you intend to keep interviewing on Saturday and Sunday?"

"Yes, sometimes the best information is gained on a person's normal off day. People are more relaxed on their off day naturally and therefore are more talkative. This is a trick I learned while serving twenty years with the Atlanta police department."

"Doc, you're full of surprises."

"You ain't seen nothing yet."

"Don't forget, call if you need anything."

"Thanks."

Woody felt extremely good about the investigation and spent the remainder of the day working on personnel matters. Just as Woody was about to leave the Chairman called and asked, "How is everything going?"

"I talked to Doc earlier and he says

everything is going good."

"I'll be at home all weekend and if you need me call on my private number."

Woody checked his notebook to be sure he had the number handy and thanked the Chairman for his concern. Woody thought, "This guy is a genuine leader."

33

Everything went fine through the weekend. There were no problems at the motel, on the road, or at the complex. Monday morning rolled around and Woody arrived at the complex on schedule at 7:00. He had worked hard all weekend and cleared his desk of paperwork. For the first time since he had been at Bakersfield, all bills were paid and all correspondence had been answered.

Lawrance called Woody and asked if he could have a seven-day extension to prepare his reply to Mr. Rawlins.

"If you make the request in writing, I will forward it to Mr. Rawlins." About an hour later Lawrance appeared at the entrance to the administrative office with his hand-written request.

"Tell Lawrance that a decision won't be made until late tomorrow and I'll notify him shortly thereafter. Have him leave a phone number where he can be reached."

Woody called Simon Rawlins and read the letter to him recommending that an extension be granted.

"I agree and you have my verbal permission to call Lawrance and inform him."

"I'll call him tomorrow about twenty-four hours from now."

Just as Woody hung up his phone rang again. The Chairman was calling. "I assume everything went okay over the weekend. I didn't hear from you."

"The plan is almost complete. Have you talked to Doc this morning?"

"No, but I plan to get an update from him by noon. Would you like to take a trip since everything is going so smoothly? I need you to check something out at another complex."

"Yes, but do I have time to drive there and back?"

"No, no, I'll send the jet to pick you and Jay Cee up tomorrow morning and bring you back before dark."

"Great. We'll be at the airport at 7:00. If anything changes, one of us will call you." This was great. Woody would be able to take Jay Cee on the trip and show him how successful he had been in his professional career.

The next morning when Woody and Jay Cee arrived at the airport the corporate jet was ready for them to board. Woody was excited and hurried Jay Cee on board and in ten minutes they were airborne, flying west over the Mississippi River.

Within thirty-five minutes they were on the ground at OBM's newest major multi-purpose complex. Woody introduced Jay Cee to the manager who had been a college dorm mate of Woody's. They had been friends for seventeen years. Jay Cee was glad to see another long-time acquaintance of Woody's and began to talk about some of the good times they had on the banks of the Sunflower River thirty years earlier.

Woody and Jay Cee had been on the ground for about three hours when Woody received a call to come to the administrative office. The receptionist said, "A lady called looking for you. She didn't leave a number, but said it was urgent that she talk to you as soon as possible." Woody had been in the office not more than fifteen minutes before the lady called again.

"Someone else is on an extension with us. You don't know us, and don't attempt to identify us now or later should an occasion arise. We have information about Lawrance Wilson that would be beneficial to OBM."

"How did you know where I was?"

"We keep an eye on you and know where you are at all times. If we get interrupted before this conversation is finished, don't leave the phone. I'll call back."

The tone of this conversation was becoming more serious and tense. Woody was trying to develop a mental picture of the person speaking. The voice sounded like a white female in her mid-thirties. Woody didn't know if the voice was disguised to fit that profile or was in fact a white female.

She continued to caution Woody never to reveal her identity and stated that if identified she and her friend on the extension would suffer considerable physical and emotional trauma. She wanted to know when Woody would return to the complex.

He said, "Later today. Can you tell me what is so urgent that you had to call long distance?"

"We just needed to talk to you as soon as possible."

"Are either of you in physical danger at the moment?"

"No, but we need to give you some information." Her voice was hesitant and shaky as if she were constantly looking around to see if someone was listening. At times she was not audible and seemed to be turning her mouth away from the phone. Woody didn't know if she was doing this to try to disguise her voice. As she talked he listened very carefully.

Woody made notes and identified the voices on his pad as Caller 1 and Caller 2. After several minutes of conversation he thought he recognized the voices. He was certain he had talked to them before, both on the phone and face to face. Caller 1 sounded like Lawrance's wife, Juanita, and Caller 2 sounded like Jacqueline Brick. They continued to tell Woody about situations involving Lawrance and other women. Caller 1 said she knew about the babysitter encounters. The voice that sounded like Juanita said, "I love Lawrance and will never give him up. I'll never confront him with the cheating and womanizing. He was like that in high school, college, and has been all of his married life. I, like so many others, am hung up on him."

The description she was giving reminded Woody of a cult relationship. Caller 2 also said, "I know about Lawrance's involvement with other women at OBM. I'm close friends with two of them and want to do whatever I can to help my friends."

Roberta and Bobbie Sue had both told Woody about the office antics of Lawrance and Jacqueline. They would frequently leave the office during the day and meet in Red Bluff at a rent-by-the-hour room motel. Roberta, being the ever-efficient timekeeper, questioned Lawrance about Jacqueline's absences. He always covered for her, telling Roberta that Jacqueline was on a special assignment for him. Roberta always smiled at that comment and said, "Yes, I know what kind of assignment she's on." Lawrance became infuriated each time Roberta made such comments and told her to keep her mouth shut or else. Caller 2 began to take the conversation away from 1. It sounded like she was getting angry with Caller 1 and apparently did not like the statement, "I love him and will never give him up."

Caller 2 said, "I hear a car coming up the driveway." Caller 1 must have looked outside, she said Lawrance had driven up and they asked Woody if he wanted to know more.

Woody answered, "Yes."

"Meet us tonight at the roadside rest

area ten miles below the metroplex."

"I'll be there if you promise to show up with some specific charges. I'm not interested in lust arrangements."

"We'll be there at 10 o'clock tonight." They were getting nervous and wanted to get off the phone. "Don't disappoint us, be there at 10 o'clock." The line went dead.

Woody sat there for a few more minutes jotting down notes from the conversation. Then he rejoined Jay Cee and continued their visit to the complex. About 4:00 they said their good-byes and headed for the airport. Jay Cee could tell Woody had something on his mind, but did not ask until they were on the plane. Woody related what had happened.

"I need to use the plane's phone to make security arrangements with our associates in the metroplex. I'm concerned that this could be a trap set by Lawrance."

"Jay Cee, if this is a trap, those two women are excellent actresses. Regardless, I agree we need to be prepared."

When they landed, Jay Cee and Woody

called the Chairman and reported the phone call. They discussed whether or not the 10 o'clock appointment should be kept and decided to go ahead if security could be provided. The Chairman agreed and said, "Call me later tonight to report what happens."

Jay Cee and Woody left the airport headed for the motel. Woody wanted to take a shower and suggested that they meet at the Red Lobster restaurant on Highway 51 at the metroplex city limits. The drive took forty-five minutes, leaving plenty of time to eat and return to the rest stop by 9:45. Woody followed Jay Cee to the rest area and parked on the lower ramp as Jay Cee drove through to check everything out. If all looked good, he would park at the northwest corner, walk through the breezeway in the visitor center and look around. That would be Woody's signal to move to the southwest corner of the parking lot where he would be in full view at all times. Everything went fine and Woody parked at the agreed upon spot shortly before 10:00 p.m.

The car he was driving had reclining

seats so Woody lowered the back about halfway so that he could stretch his legs and be more comfortable. The night air was cool and the temperature in the car cooled quickly. He sat in position until 11 o'clock. No one appeared and he was getting a little agitated, so at 11:30 he got out of the car and went to the restroom in the visitor center. The cool night air chilled him.

By 12:30 he was tired and sleepy and decided to drive to the nearest coffee shop to help him wake up. He wondered what had happened to the lady callers.

Did Lawrance find out about their plan? Did they decide not to come? Were they just pulling a trick on Woody? Jay Cee left the rest stop behind Woody and followed him to the coffee shop. They discussed what to do. Should Woody return to the motel or go back to the rest stop and wait some more?

"I really want to give them an opportunity to contact me because I detected a note of desperation in their voices."

"I think we should leave, they're not going to show."

"I believe the callers and I think if we wait a little longer they'll show up. I'm really more interested in who they are than what they have to say. I want to go back to the rest stop and wait another hour or two before leaving."

"Okay, you lead. If there are any cars parked there ignore them and go to the same parking spot." Woody agreed and they left the coffee shop.

When Woody returned to the rest area, one car was in the parking lot. It was parked in a space in the middle and as Woody pulled by he noticed that it had an out-of-state license. Woody pulled into the same spot he had previously occupied, adjusted the seat and relaxed. The night was getting cooler and Woody was getting very tired.

He sat there for a few minutes and began to doze. He had been up since 5:30 that morning and had a fast and furious day of activity. Woody didn't know what Jay Cee was doing but wondered if he might also fall asleep.

About 3:00 a.m. Woody was awakened by something bumping the car. He raised up and saw something stuck under the windshield wiper on the driver's side. As he looked around the parking lot, he saw Jay Cee's car in the same location and also a second car parked directly in line between them. As Woody looked at the paper on the windshield, he realized that the other car was blocking Jay Cee's view, so he stopped to analyze the situation. Rather than opening the car door, he decided to start the engine and move closer to the visitor center. He picked a spot directly under an overhead light. With the engine running and the car still in park, he quickly stepped out and removed the paper. The overhead light was so bright he could easily read the note while sitting in the car. It said, "We were here. We wanted to test you to see if you would cooperate with us. We will contact you later." Woody was infuriated.

He jerked the car out of park and started toward Jay Cee, who had been watching and had his car cranked and ready to leave. Woody turned in front of Jay Cee and headed to the exit. They drove straight to the motel. Woody could not believe he had given up a night's sleep for a typewritten note that produced nothing of interest.

When Woody reached his room he called Jay Cee and told him what was in the note and that he was sorry that they had to spend the night cramped in the front seat of their cars. Jay Cee said, "Well, you never know what stakeouts will turn up. A lot of time is spent sitting and waiting with no apparent results. Sometimes you think you're wasting your time but, by being where you are supposed to be you encourage informants to come forward later. Informants are usually weak, fearful people. They need to feel comfortable. So don't be discouraged."

Woody had shown the informants they could trust him to be good to his word. Jay Cee said, "The informants are in Lawrance's camp, walking a tight rope trying to provide information and at the same time not arouse suspicion."

All this police psychology lecture was interesting to Woody but he was still steamed about being stood up. Jay Cee said, "You were not stood up. You just didn't get the type information you expected. Calm down, take a cold shower, and go to bed."

"By the time I take a shower it will be time to go to work."

"Call Roberta about 6:30 a.m. and tell her you will be a little late coming to work. You need to get some sleep."

"Yeah, that's a good idea." There was nothing pressing at the office since most of the overdue paperwork had been taken care of two days before. "Will you call the Chairman and tell him of our change in plans?"

"Roger, boss, I'll take care of that detail. You take a shower and call Roberta."

34

Woody had no problem sleeping soundly until Jay Cee woke him at 11:00 to get up and go to work. Although not fully recovered from the night before, Woody felt rested and ready to go.

He arrived at the complex and started reviewing the safety record of each employee. Bobbie Sue asked, "Do you intend to conduct any more employee interviews?"

He responded, "No." Since Doc was interviewing them, he would suspend his interviews until Doc was finished.

"The interviews are having a positive impact on the work force. I've heard several employees say they are glad to get back to their real jobs because they know what to expect and enjoy their work."

"The next manager can continue; I need to turn my attention to other matters. The most important thing is to be sure the employees perform only the duties OBM hired them to do."

"Working here may be fun again if Lawrance never returns."

"I don't see any possible way Lawrance can ever return to his old job. He should be more worried about staying out of jail than reassuming his position with OBM."

"Are there any plans to press criminal charges?"

"The Chairman told me he would exert all the effort OBM could muster to send Lawrance to prison. He wants to send a message to all employees who may be inclined to violate the law and wants Lawrance to spend some time behind bars. Although I have known the Chairman only three years, my experience is once he sets his mind on a course of action, he will see it through to a satisfactory conclusion."

"I have met him only once and he impressed me as a no-nonsense type."

Woody agreed with Bobbie Sue's characterization and thanked her for her assistance and concern. He then turned to the task at hand.

Bobbie Sue interrupted and said, "I have some payment documents you need to sign. I'll bring them to your office in a few minutes."

"Okay." After about fifteen minutes the phone rang breaking the quietness and Woody's concentration. Jay Cee was calling to tell Woody that the security team had found the pickup. Jay Cee asked Woody to meet him in front of the Red Lobster where they had eaten a couple of nights ago.

"I'll meet you there in forty-five minutes on one condition: that you stop somewhere and get us some sandwiches and drinks for lunch."

"Fine, but don't waste any time."

"I have a couple of things to do that won't take long and I'll meet you in front of the restaurant as soon as I can." Woody called Roberta and asked if she needed anything because he would be out of the office for the rest of the day.

She said, "I have some bonus checks that need your signature, but they can wait until tomorrow."

"Great, have all recipients come to the executive conference room tomorrow morning at 8:00, and we will have a little ceremony."

"We've never done anything like that before."

"Fine, things are changing for the better. Have the photographer here and have someone prepare an article for the newspaper." He planned to use this occasion to boost morale as high as possible. "Let's move the ceremony to the training room and have all employees attend."

"We don't have enough chairs."

"Don't worry. Tell Tommy to have all the chairs removed. I don't want anybody seated. They need to move around and talk, reminiscent of a family reunion."

"Have you lost your mind?"

"No, but if I do you'll be the first to know."

The reaction Woody got from Roberta was not expected, but it surely was rewarding.

Woody drove around the square until he saw Jay Cee's vehicle parked near the entrance to the restaurant. He parked, got out, and headed toward Jay Cee who walked away from his car and motioned for Woody to follow down a side street. As Woody entered the side street he saw a big travel van with dark windows. Jay Cee called to him to hurry up. Woody shook his head because he never knew what to expect when Jay Cee made the arrangements. When Woody entered the vehicle he was surprised to see the security team who had taken him to dinner one night. One said, "We've been working with local authorities and found a truck fitting the description Jay Cee gave us. We want you to take a look and see if it looks like the one that bumped you."

They drove for about fifteen minutes back toward the complex. The pickup they were looking for was parked in front of the house that belonged to Leggs Redmond. As the van stopped in front of the house, one of the men got out to inspect the tires. Woody and Jay Cee looked at the truck while one of the women took photographs. She had a camera with a zoom lens that could zero in on the tiniest speck of chipped paint or spread out to provide a full view.

The truck was parked facing the house. Jay Cee was able to identify the rear end as the one he saw leaving the motel parking area, but Woody was not sure. The security team quickly devised a scheme whereby the photographer could get a front view of the pickup. She and a male agent walked up to the house and knocked on the door. A middle-aged black woman appeared at the screen door and as the man talked to her through the screen, the photographer took photos of the front of the truck with a hidden camera in her briefcase. After a couple of minutes they returned to the van. The pictures developed instantly and after looking at them, Woody positively identified the truck as the one that had bumped him on that dark rainy night about a month earlier.

As they drove away from the house, the other male agent picked up the mobile phone and placed a call to the metroplex requesting that action be taken to have local authorities impound the truck. Woody and Jay Cee were sitting back enjoying this ride and watching this group of highly trained professionals work.

Woody asked, "Where is my lunch?"

Jay Cee opened the oven and said, "Do you want hamburgers or hot dogs?"

Woody laughed and said, "One of each with mustard, pickle, lettuce, but no mayonnaise. Remember my elevated cholesterol."

"Yes, I remember and these hamburgers and hot dogs are low-fat too." A few minutes later the van returned Woody and Jay Cee to their cars. Woody thanked his four accomplices once again, got in his car, and headed toward the motel. As Woody stopped at a service station to get gas, Jay Cee pulled in behind him and parked near the restrooms. Woody filled the tank, then went to the restroom to wash his hands. He asked Jay Cee if he wanted to stop by Doc's interrogation room for a while.

"Yes, call Sara and tell her we are on the way."

Woody made the call and Sara asked, "Where in the heck have you been? We have some really interesting statements and want to share them with you."

"We'll be there in ten minutes."

She asked if Jay Cee might have a disguise he could put on to pose as a "white dude."

Woody turned to Jay Cee and asked if he were equipped.

"Yes, without a doubt." Woody told Sara it would take about twenty minutes to get prepared so she could expect them in thirty minutes. She said the door would be left unlocked and for them to enter quietly. Although she and Doc had finished interviewing for the day, she did not want to call any undue attention to her room.

When they got to Sara's room she and Doc were seated on the sofa. Doc as usual was talking and feeling good. Sara went to the bar and set a bottle of wine on the counter along with four glasses. She invited them to have a glass while they sat and talked. She, just like Doc, seemed to be elated. Woody kept looking at

Jay Cee with a quizzical look. The vibes told Woody this was going to be extremely good news. And it was.

The incriminating evidence the Chairman had been looking for was now contained in four sworn statements. Sara said, "I've discussed this evidence with the U.S. Attorney's Office and they agree that sufficient evidence has been gathered to press criminal charges against Lawrance, the deputy, Leggs and the whole gang. They are going to wait for OBM to finish its investigation then subpoena all records related to this case." Sara explained that the information Doc had gathered would make an easy case for the Justice Department to prosecute.

Woody asked Doc to explain what hard evidence he had uncovered and from which employees. Doc declined and said, "I'll tell the Chairman first and if he gives the okay, I'll tell you. All you two need to know at this point is the case is solid." Doc said all the employees feared for their jobs if they refused to follow Lawrance's orders. They knew it was wrong, but what could they do? "I assured each interviewee that he had the right and would retain the right to refuse to do something illegal as long as he worked for OBM."

Woody and Jay Cee left Sara's room about 11:00 p.m. They arrived at the motel before midnight and went directly to their rooms. Woody told Jay Cee to go to his window and watch the group of people assembled across the parking lot.

Jay Cee asked, "Do you recognize any of them?"

"Yes, but I don't know their names."

Jay Cee went to the top of the motel with his special night vision camera. He was able to get several clear photographs of the group and wanted to have them identified as soon as possible. Woody said, "Roberta can probably identify them and we can make an overlay with names matching faces."

Woody chuckled and told Jay Cee he hoped he was as good a photographer as The Kid. The subjects definitely were not as interesting as the ones in The Kid's photographs.

Woody said he was tired and wanted to go to sleep. Jay Cee agreed and bid his friend good night.

35

The next morning Woody arrived at the complex at 7:00. He met Billy Mack on the road. Billy turned around and pulled into a parking spot next to Woody. They always kidded each other about how their vegetable gardens were growing. Both bragged and stretched the truth a little bit. Woody commented that his garden would have to grow under Joseph's watchful eye. Joseph had been interested in gardening and especially loved to plant beans and corn. Once as Joseph sat on Woody's broad shoulders while they walked through the tall corn, the little boy told his dad, "That's some mighty fine corn." Woody loved to tell this story and took a lot of pride each time he told it.

Billy Mack said, "Well, since you won't be able to have your own garden this year, I'll keep you in fresh vegetables."

Woody thanked him. "I'm sure I will enjoy them."

Woody went to his office and worked undisturbed for about three hours. He had forgotten about the pictures Jay Cee had taken the night before. Bobbie Sue stopped at the office and said, "I just made a fresh pot of coffee. Do you want a cup?" Woody thanked her but declined. Roberta heard the conversation from her office and joined in.

Seeing Roberta jogged Woody's memory of the photos. He asked her to look at them and identify as many of the subjects as she could. After a quick glance at the pictures, she said, "I know all of them."

Woody said, "Great. Please make me an overlay identifying names with faces."

"No problem," and left Woody's office. In less than fifteen minutes she returned, mission accomplished. "All these employees are in the last interview group for Doc. This is the group most loyal to Lawrance. Where did you get these?"

"It just came into my possession this morning."

"Well okay, don't tell me." Woody said maybe later. She returned to her office and continued to process personnel papers.

About 11:30 Woody's phone rang. Doc and Sara were on the other end and wanted to know if Woody had heard the latest about the mysterious pickup. Woody said, "I heard that the local authorities were supposed to impound it this morning."

"The pickup has disappeared."

"Has anyone contacted Jay Cee or the Chairman?"

"No."

"I'll get in touch with them immediately to let them know what's going on." Woody went to the pay phone and called the Chairman who patched Jay Cee into the conversation. Woody told them the pickup had disappeared.

Jay Cee was furious and said, "I'll call

the metroplex security and get them to check with the local sheriff's office. They'll sort through this situation and keep me informed. I'll keep you, Doc, and Sara up to date as soon as I find out something."

They finished the conversation and Woody returned to the complex. He didn't hear anything regarding the pickup until about 4:30 when Jay Cee called and said, "They have a lead, and I'll fill you in when you get to the motel." Woody immediately left the office driving faster than the speed limit because he was anxious to hear the news. He arrived at the motel, parked, and rushed to his room.

Jay Cee arrived at Woody's room within two minutes and said, "My security connection in the metroplex has proved a conspiracy involving Lawrance, the sheriff's deputy, and Leggs. The deputy was picked up by the U.S. Marshals and the FBI and transported out of this county to be jailed. The FBI investigators are questioning him and feel certain they'll break his story in short order. The sheriff has been directed to pick up Leggs for questioning;

Lawrance is under surveillance but is allowed to move about freely. The U.S. Marshals hope he will lead them to the pickup. If he does, they'll have a direct connection between him, the bumping incident, and the rock thrown through your window."

The separation of the suspects during interrogations would surely produce additional incriminating evidence against Lawrance. Jay Cee said, "I've already briefed the Chairman tonight and will keep him posted as events occur." Jay Cee told Woody one of them needed to stay by the phone. He suggested that Woody go to the restaurant, eat supper, and return. Then Jay Cee could go eat while Woody sat by the phone.

After they had taken turns eating, they were sitting in Jay Cee's room talking and watching television when the phone rang. It was the security team from the metroplex calling with good news. With the assistance of an FBI investigator, the sheriff had gotten a full confession from Leggs. Leggs asked for immunity and was granted it pending his providing evidence that linked Lawrance to their illegal activities. Leggs agreed to the deal and told the FBI investigator that Lawrance had ordered him to put the rattlesnake in Woody's car and also threatened to kill him if he did not cooperate and do Lawrance's dirty work. Leggs was describing the time he tried to force Woody off the road and the rock throwing incident that shattered Woody's motel room window. Leggs said, "Mr. Lawrance threatened violence against me and my family. He told me he would have the mob from the city wipe out my entire family if I didn't cooperate." Leggs was so intimidated he saw no alternative other than to follow Lawrance's orders. During the confession, he expressed sorrow for causing Woody problems.

Woody and Jay Cee called the Chairman again and reported the latest news regarding Leggs. The Chairman said that he would have his chief lawyer contact the U.S. Attorney to draw up the necessary documents to begin criminal proceedings against Lawrance.

36

Word spread quickly. When Woody arrived at the complex the next morning, five employees met him in the parking lot. They wanted to know what was going to happen to Leggs. Woody replied, "It's out of my hands. Our lawyers are looking at various options." Woody reminded them that if they cooperated fully with Doc during their interviews, penalties would be less severe. As a result, three of them asked if they could talk to Doc again. Woody asked, "Why do you want to see him again?"

One responded, "I forgot to tell him some things."

"Do you remember everything now?

What has caused you to have a sudden remembrance?"

"I was just nervous, but I remember now."

Woody told them he would call Doc and set up the appointments. Woody went to his office and asked Bobbie Sue to bring him a cup of coffee. He invited her to have a seat and tell him what she had heard. She said, "Rumors are rampant throughout the county. Someone told me Lawrance was arrested and sent to jail in Pike County. They also said Leggs has been shipped out of state to a federal prison, and a county deputy has been fired."

Woody chuckled, "Isn't it strange how rumors get started?"

"You haven't heard anything?"

"Yes, I've heard some of those rumors but I don't believe them yet."

"Yet? Does that mean anything in particular? What are you waiting for — a front page headline in the local newspaper?"

"I'm waiting on someone in authority to tell me before I believe anything."

Roberta entered Woody's office saying, "Several employees want to see you."

"What do they want?"

"They want to talk to Doc."

"About what?"

"They want to change their statements."

"Okay, send them in." The five employees who stopped him that morning in the parking area were accompanied by six more. He invited them to come in and sit down, then asked, "What's this all about?"

The same employee who spoke in the parking area had been appointed by the group to be the spokesman. Woody looked around the room, and to his amazement, discovered that this was the same group that Jay Cee had photographed a couple of nights earlier. Woody pulled one of the photographs out of his desk, passed it around, and asked, "Do any of you see yourself?"

A hush fell over the room as each employee looked at the photo. The spokesman was stone silent. Woody asked, "Do any of you want to tell me where you were when this picture was taken?"

They began to shuffle and clear their throats. One of them finally spoke. He said, "We were outside your motel room."

"Why were you sitting in the parking area at the motel?"

"Mr. Lawrance told us to."

"Told you to do what?"

"We were there to scare you and make you leave."

"Well, it didn't work, did it?"

"No sir."

"If I get you another appointment with Doc, are you going to tell him everything this time?"

They all replied, "Yes sir."

"If you lied on your sworn statements before, how do I know you won't lie this time?"

"No sir, we won't this time."

"If you don't tell the truth this time, you will lose your jobs."

They all said they understood and would tell Lawrance they were going to tell the truth. Woody asked Roberta to call Tommy to the office. When he arrived Woody said, "These men will not be available to work their evening shift. They have requested another audience with Doc." Woody asked Tommy to canvass the entire work force to see if anyone else wanted to talk to Doc again. Woody reminded Tommy to tell everybody this was the last opportunity OBM would give them to tell the truth. "If anyone has sworn to a lie, then they had better take this opportunity to get the record straight. After this round, no more statements will be taken."

Tommy said, "Yes sir." Less than an hour later he returned with the names of sixteen employees who wanted to have another interview with Doc.

Woody asked, "Did you contact all the employees?"

"Yes sir, these sixteen want to change or add to their previous statements."

"Do you have anything you want to change?"

"No sir, I don't need to change anything, but I do want to add some additional comments."

"Give the list to Roberta and she will set up the time and provide you a schedule."

Tommy was extremely shaken by this turn of events. He told Woody he wanted to get everything out in the open this time. No more holding back. He said, "I realize my future with OBM depends on reestablishing my loyalty. I'm tired of covering for Mr. Lawrance. He used me and now I want to testify in court against him. Regardless of what my future holds, I want to come clean and I hope OBM will find a place for me."

Woody assured him that total cooperation would help his chances tremendously. Tommy extended his hand to Woody and said, "Thank you for explaining all this mess to me and for allowing me to keep my job during the investigation. No matter what happens from this point on, I will always believe you are a fair man with the people and company's best interest at heart." Woody assured him he was concerned about both. Tommy left the office and closed the door behind him. Woody called Doc and told him what had happened. Doc agreed to conduct the additional interviews and said, "I'll be ready whenever they arrive."

It took Doc two days to complete the sixteen additional interviews. Each one took longer than the first time since each interviewee was more cooperative and talkative and not hostile. The employees provided detailed information complete with specific dates and times. After Doc completed all of the interviews he called Woody to thank him for his cooperation.

"I've never seen such a dramatic change in a group of people in my twenty years of investigating." Doc was pensive in his comments and left the impression that he felt sorry for the sixteen individuals. The information they provided put the last nail in Lawrance Wilson's coffin. When the U.S. Attorneys put this information with other evidence already in hand, they would undoubtedly begin criminal proceedings against Lawrance. In addition to the powerful written statements, each person had volunteered to testify against the man who had wrecked so many lives.

Doc suggested that the "white hat" gang get together one last time. He asked Woody to contact their security assistants in the metroplex and extend an invitation to all of those who provided the basic factual material in the first interview. Their knowledge and willingness to cooperate gave Doc the necessary ammunition that allowed him to use his investigative techniques supported by fact and sprinkled with pressure to pry incriminating statements out of groups four, five, and six.

Woody told Doc that he would be happy to contact everyone and make the arrangements. "Is Saturday night at 7:00 okay?"

"Yes, I have only one more detail to take care of. I have to write a summary report for the Chairman, CEO and SEO. It will take me at least a day to write it. Is the offer for typing support still open?"

"Absolutely. Would you prefer to dictate rather than write the report?"

"That's an excellent idea."

"Roberta will be available at your request to do the typing."

"Thanks a lot, send her to the interrogation room at 8:00 a.m. tomorrow."

"She will be there ready to go to work."

Woody hung up the phone, leaned back in his chair, closed his eyes, and reflected on the events of the past month. It was hard to believe that so many dramatic and traumatic situations had occurred in such a short time. His mind drifted toward thoughts of his family. He longed for a reunion with them and planned to go on a real vacation just as soon as a new manager was appointed to the Bakersfield complex.

Doc finished his reports and sent copies to the Chairman, Chief Executive Officer, and Senior Executive Officer. After reviewing the documents with his chief lawyer, the SEO contacted Doc and told him to provide copies to the U.S. Attorneys within twenty-four hours. Doc said, "I'll contact the Attorney's office and make the necessary appointment." He was pleased that the SEO had approved his reports and had given him the opportunity to personally deliver copies of his findings to the prosecutor.

Doc contacted Mr. Jeb Nosam, Chief Attorney, and set up a meeting. Jeb said, "I'm looking forward to your visit and will have the preliminary documents required by the U.S. District Judge, Clementine Rushmore, prepared and ready when you get here. My office will do everything in our power to expedite this case and bring it to trial."

When Doc arrived for the meeting, Jeb and a staff member quickly added Doc's findings to their package of documents. In less than thirty minutes Jeb and Doc were headed for Judge Rushmore's District Court in Red Bluff. When they arrived in the Judge's chambers, they were met by Strick Stephland, Court Clerk. Strick said, "I'm glad to see you and hope you have everything in order. As you know, I've been interested in this case since it was first brought to my attention. Lawrance Wilson has an intriguing reputation in this community and I'm looking forward to a trial so that some rumors can be aired in the courtroom. If half the stories are true, Hollywood could make a box office hit out of them."

Jeb said, "I hope the Judge's calendar is not too full."

Strick said, "I believe I can get Her Honor to sign an order before noon today. Lawrance should be in Federal custody within the next twenty-four hours."

Jeb thanked Strick for his assistance and asked to be kept informed of all developments. Strick said, "As soon as I know something, I'll let you know."

Jeb and Doc left the Judge's chambers in a euphoric mood. "I've got to make a phone call." Doc called the Chairman and told him the documents had been delivered to Judge Rushmore and action to pick up Lawrance would be taken immediately.

The Chairman said, "Good work, Doc. You've done an excellent job and I'll make certain you are rewarded."

"Woody McKenzie made my job a lot easier and should also be rewarded for his efforts and hard work. He held the work force together and made sure that the field organization continued to function even after he and his family were in danger."

"I agree and will contact Woody immediately and pass this information on."

"I'll also contact Woody. We are planning on getting several people at the complex together tonight for a celebration."

"Doc, don't celebrate too much. You must remember that you, Woody, and others will have to testify during the trial and we wouldn't want anyone to think that we have accomplished our goal. I'll consider us successful only when Lawrance is behind bars facing a long jail sentence."

"Don't worry, all we have to do is let the legal system work. Although Lawrance is not in Federal custody at this moment, it is just a matter of time before he is incarcerated to await trial."

37

With Lawrance in custody, Woody devoted his attention to his boyhood friend — turned protector. They had recently talked about getting their families together for a reunion at Woody's ole home place.

Woody knew his parents would be overjoyed to see both Jay Cee and Ida Bee. Although Ida Bee had left the McKenzie family under strained circumstances, the warm motherly feeling for her remained as strong as ever in Ethel's heart. Woody remembered with pleasure the relationship that existed among the three families when they lived within an easy walking mile of each other. It would be a wonderful reunion if they could all get together and talk about "the good ole days." Woody and his mother frequently reminisced about their experiences and fun times with the Williams and Whitaker families. Ethel told Woody she often dreamed of a reunion with her old friends.

Now Woody had the opportunity to make his mother's dream come true and he could not think of a better way to thank Jay Cee for his help and support during their most recent trying and dangerous time.

Although they had encountered their share of dangerous childhood situations, no one would have ever expected they would be confronted with the life and death circumstance they had faced at Bakersfield. Woody leaned forward, picked up the phone, and dialed Jay Cee's home number. He hoped Ida Bee would answer so he could play a game of "guess who's calling." Jay Cee, however, answered the phone and immediately recognized Woody's voice. The "frig man" said, "Man, I just got resettled at home. I hope you're not in trouble again."

Woody laughed. "Do you think I only call

you when I'm in trouble?"

"Well, that's the way it's been lately."

You could hear the happiness in Woody's voice as he countered, "Ole buddy, you're wrong this time. I want you and Ida Bee to come visit us as soon as you can."

EPILOGUE

THE ODE OF THE BAKERSFIELD FIVE

White hats come and white hats go
A mystery to us, for we will never know
Why Sam, Simon, and Tony continue to resist
Could it be because we persist?
And as the last hope seems to disappear the
"Sheriff" in his despair calls
"Sir, come here"
Could it be White Hat Bill?
The last tin-star hero who will
He will pull up his trousers as a man
And not be afraid to take command
White hats come and white hats go
But it is for sure that this one will stay and show
This cast of players assembled here
Shall go forward this day without fear
This action will not fail
Because truth and right will prevail
The moral of the story is quite clear
When things are not going so nifty
Just pull out your trusty B.A.R. 600-50

B. J. Woods
© 21 Mar 91

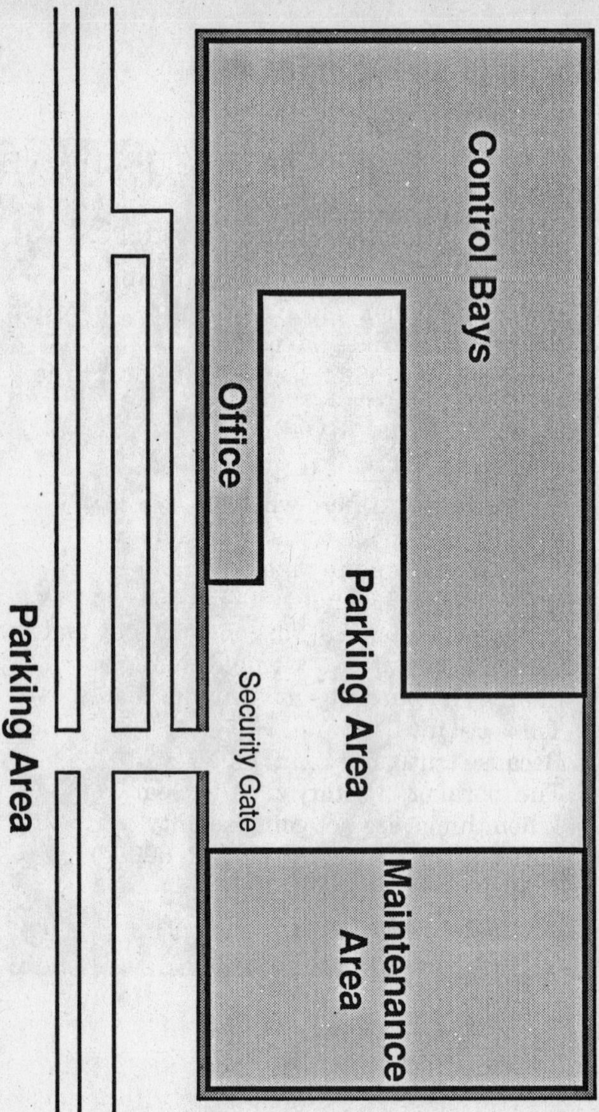
Control Bays
Office
Parking Area
Security Gate
Maintenance Area
Parking Area

WHERE THE FERRY CROSSES

BAKERSFIELD MOTEL

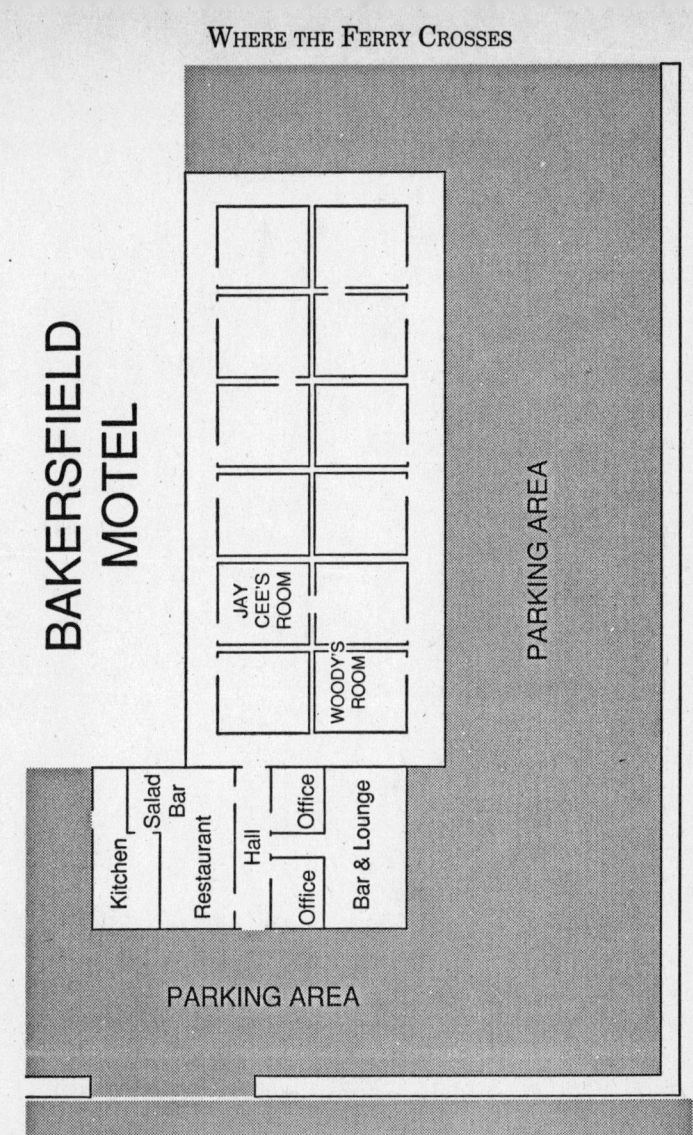

- JAY CEE'S ROOM
- WOODY'S ROOM
- Kitchen
- Salad Bar
- Restaurant
- Hall
- Office
- Office
- Bar & Lounge

PARKING AREA

PARKING AREA

TO BAKERSFIELD

429

B.J. Woods is a native Mississippian and with the exception of two years has spent his entire life living and working in the southeast. From his childhood years in the Mississippi Delta where living conditions consisted of the bare essentials for survival through his formal education and successful professional career he has experienced a broad spectrum of economic situations and human behavior.

Heart surgery in 1992 forced the author to slow his busy pace and gave him time to concentrate on writing. *Where The Ferry Crosses* is his first novel.